The Bookstore of Other Languages

A NOVEL

Victoria Josslin

Victoria Josslin/E.F. Metz Press
183 A Wallace Way NE
Bainbridge Island, Washington 98110-1829
www.victoriajosslin.com

Publisher's Note: This is a work of fiction. Names, characters, places, and incidents are a product of the author's imagination. Locales and public names are sometimes used for atmospheric purposes. Any resemblance to actual people, living or dead, or to businesses, companies, events, institutions, or locales is completely coincidental.

Book Layout © 2017 BookDesignTemplates.com
Cover design Jeanette Alexander
Cover art © 1997 Victoria Josslin

The Bookstore of Other Languages/ Victoria Josslin. -- 1st ed.
ISBN 978-1-7320945-0-5

Acknowledgements

This book is very different from and much better than its first draft, thanks to the careful observaions and suggestions of Bev Young, Jim Demetre, Gail Ringel, Carolyn Terry, and Jeanie Murphy.

Developmental editor Jenn Hager tore into the Bookstore with energy and enthusiasm, catching many woeful errors, and helping me believe that the novel and I were both for real. Jeanette Alexander designed the beautiful cover. Grateful thanks to you both.

It could go without saying that David Margolin's confidence in me was my foundation, but I say it anyway.

"To have another language is to possess a second soul."

–CHARLEMAGNE, HOLY ROMAN EMPEROR (742-814)

CONTENTS

CHAPTER ONE

I'm going to die.

Well, duh, of course you're going to die. Everybody dies.

No, but really, I'm going to die soon!

You don't know that, you have to calm down and wait. Dr. Valerie said it was probably nothing.

She's being a tactful professional. What do you think? She's going to tell me the bad news herself? No, she's going to wait and let a stranger tell me. After a few months of agonizing and disgusting treatment, I'm going to die.

Bryce had repeated variations on this interior dialogue for two weeks, ever since mid-January when he had gone to the Eliza Island Clinic and kept his annual appointment with Dr. Valerie Lucas. Dr. Valerie always looked alarmingly lean and healthy – she was a dedicated runner, and it seemed to Bryce that whenever he drove to a customer's house, in whatever weather, he saw her running by the side of the road in her reflective gear. She expected her patients to keep healthy, too.

Dr. Valerie came in the exam room, test results in hand. "Everything looks pretty good," she said. "But you know," and she looked at him over her reading glasses, "everything would be a bit better if you got more exercise and lost a few pounds."

Bryce winced. "I know."

"Think you could increase your daily exercise by ten percent?"

"It wouldn't take much to increase zero by ten percent."

She gave him the look over the reading glasses again.

He lowered his head and looked down at his belly. "Okay," he said. "That's probably a good idea."

"It is. Cutting back calories by ten percent would be an even better idea."

He shrugged. She raised her eyebrows.

"Right. Yes. Okay."

She listened to his lungs, looked in his throat, and gently felt under his jaw.

"You have a lump," she said.

"Are you telling me that I'm sad and I have a lump in my throat and I need to see a therapist?" he asked.

"No, I'm telling you that you have a lump in your neck and you need to see an ENT in Seattle," she answered. "It's probably nothing, but you need to know for sure. Want Dolores to make an appointment for you?"

Going to Seattle was a drag. When Bryce and Sheila moved to Eliza Island, they thought they'd be close enough to get to the city at least once in a while, often enough to visit the museums and galleries, to go to concerts and lectures at the university, walk around, see the sights. They could have romantic weekends in the metropolis, treat themselves to a night at a fancy hotel, try out trendy restaurants that had been reviewed in the paper, splurge on concert tickets.

A few years had taught them that it was both more complicated and more boring than they had thought. You spent hours waiting for the ferry, riding the ferry to a bigger island, waiting for another ferry, riding that ferry, then driving into town. It was expensive, too, especially in the summer when the ferry system raised its prices to soak the tourists.

Besides, island living turned out to be easier and more interesting than Bryce had thought it would be. The population was big enough that not only were there schools and grocery stores and churches and gas stations, but there was a clinic, a movie theater, a marriage counselor, a chiropractor, Lo Tengo Mexican restaurant, The Crab Pot Pub, and Mr. D's Coffee Shop with gluten-free muffins for the tourists and apple fritters for the residents. You could find almost anything that you felt like reading at Turn the Page Bookstore. There was Strung Out, a yarn and craft shop where Sheila worked. And there was Bryce's very own business, Hanford Computers, Etcetera, where the locals bought computers, phones, games, and internet connection.

Bryce enjoyed the courteous tone of day-to-day relations and came to realize that what had originally struck him as a superficial blandness was, in fact, a result of everybody knowing one another. People avoided cutting someone off in traffic because that other driver was apt to be their child's chemistry teacher, or the banker they were about to ask for a loan, or just somebody they had a crush on. Bryce was not so foolish as to assume that people were equally restrained in their private lives, but he was grateful for the daily civility.

And there was the house, an old summer home brought up to date in a new way each decade for over eighty years. It pleased Bryce enormously that the house had been allowed to evolve over time rather than torn down and replaced. Indoor plumbing had arrived, then electricity, and later the insulation that had turned it into a year-rounder. Bryce's persistent weekend efforts over six years had turned the original week-end cottage into a functional and comfortable home.

While Bryce settled into island life, Sheila became increasingly restless, and finally, on a sunny day last June, she had packed her clothes, her cookbooks, her grandmother's china, her salt-and-pepper shaker collection, her pasta maker, her yarn, and her two looms into her old Subaru and took off with Woofie, the Chihuahua-poodle mix, to drive back to Portland.

I'm only thirty-eight. I'm too young to die.

Mozart wasn't too young. Bob Marley wasn't too young. Alexander the Great wasn't too young. What's so special about you?

Well, right, but they're not me! What's special about me is that I'm me!

You have to wait.

I hate waiting!

Two weeks after seeing Dr. Valerie, Bryce took the ferries and drove to Seattle to keep his appointment with Dr. Jordan Branch. Why not spring for a hotel, he had thought. We always meant to and never did. Besides, that way after I get the bad news I won't have to be brave in front of people I know on the ferry on the way home. He drove to the Toscana Hotel and checked in. Backpack in hand, he went to his room.

The windows looked east out across the city, and he felt like he was in a movie. A stranger checks into a hotel, pours himself a drink, and looks out at the soul-less city beneath him. It was too early to have a drink, though, and it seemed dumb to drink before a doctor's appointment. The doctor would smell it on his breath. Who knows what conclusion he – or she – might come to? Could Dr. Jordan Branch be a woman? Bryce asked himself if he'd rather get the bad news from a man or a woman.

Bryce went into the bathroom and looked at his image in the mirror. He decided that if he had to have chemo the first thing he would do would be to shave off his mustache. It would be so horrible to have it fall out bit by bit. He couldn't decide about when to shave his head. He stared at his hair, floppy brown waves tossed by cowlicks. He couldn't tell what he'd look like without his hair and mustache. Would his eyebrows fall out?

To hell with it, he thought, went down in the elevator, and out into a drippy Seattle February afternoon. Sullen and sweating, he trudged up the hill to St. Olaf Hospital.

After Sheila left, Bryce spent the summer building raised beds and planting vegetables. He read a new biography of Samuel Adams and then read a little more about the American Revolution. He went to the barber instead of having Sheila cut his hair. He set aside money every month, but he wasn't quite sure why. His father, Roger, visited and helped him re-plumb the bathroom. Deer ate his vegetables. In the fall he went to a pumpkin-carving party. Hanford Computers, Etc. handed out candy on Halloween. He tried baking his own bread. He spent Thanksgiving with friends.

A major software company had introduced a new operating system, and Bryce and Justin Goldsmith, his assistant, prepared to upgrade their customers to the new OS, figuring out the most obvious problems that would turn up and how to fix them. In November the new School Board decided to upgrade their IT system and had unrealistic expectations of both the cost and the anticipated improvements on their current system. Bryce met with the superintendent, and then with the Board, coaxing them down the path of reason.

As each weekend approached, Bryce drowned his sorrows in the Crab Pot, where he had been adopted by the Friday Study Group, a congenial group of high school faculty members, Hal (algebra), Ginnie (English composition and the yearbook), and Ashley (American History). He looked forward to their weekly conversations that could include local politics, travel plans, new movies, old movies, internet security, science fiction, and the complaints of daily life, all accompanied by robust Northwest microbrews.

At Christmas Bryce visited his parents in Portland, where he teased Linda, his mother, talked with Roger, his father, about everything from Manifest Destiny to bicycles in the city; he visited his sister and her family, bought presents for his nephews, kidded around with Uncle Mel, and avoided his cousin Brenda. He read more about the American Revolution and then moved to the French Revolution. In January he celebrated his thirty-eighth birthday and went in for his annual physical.

Dr. Jordan Branch, it turned out, was a woman, lean like Dr. Valerie, probably also a runner. Her hair was as you'd expect a specialist's to be – short and gray; her manners as you'd want a specialist's to be – both crisp and tender.

"Ah, well," she said. "It was a good idea to get it checked, Mr. Hanford, but this is a benign cyst. Nothing, really. We'll just aspirate it. I'll send it to the lab, but don't worry about it. If it comes back we'll treat it again, but that's not likely. You'll be good to go."

Twenty minutes later, that was that. He was fine. Except for his legs, which had suddenly become just a little unsteady. He slowly made his way to the hospital cafeteria, bought a cup of coffee and a bagel, found a quiet corner, and cautiously lowered himself into a chair. He looked at other people sitting and eating, paying no attention at all to the glorious and miraculous state of their good health. He watched as a woman with a little girl took their lunches to a table. The girl, maybe seven or eight, was dainty, dressed in pale pink. Her hair had been neatly braided into cornrows. She looked at her mother, and Bryce thought he'd never seen a smile so radiant. *Stop it!* he said to himself. *How corny are you going to get? You're not in a movie! You're not Jimmy Stewart!* He sipped his cafeteria coffee and it filled his mouth with an astonishingly rich and complex flavor. *This is stupid! I'm out of here.*

He put his parka on and left the hospital thinking that he had the rest of the day to drift through the city, enjoying its historic buildings, its flower shops, art galleries, antique stores, boutiques and nail salons, trees and manhole covers, drifting clouds and sudden views of the water. He went into a bookstore and treated himself to a new revisionist history of Texas. He wandered toward the Pike Place Market, past a gelateria, an adult movie theater, a kitchen store, and a Starbucks. A pair of buskers: a skinny, red-headed young man wearing a Mariners t-shirt and lederhosen sawed at a fiddle while a fair-skinned, blue-eyed girl with long blonde braids, wearing some vaguely Bavarian costume, plucked a mandolin. Against some part of his will, Bryce dropped a five-dollar bill into the fiddle case. He paused to enjoy the view toward the water and saw steep stairs leading down to the west, and thought "why not?" He took his time walking down the stairs, admiring the graffiti on the wall, trying to imagine what it must be like to be the person who had made these intricate, stylish, swaggering messages to the neighborhood.

He walked past a sausage shop and decided it was too early for lunch. He went past a used-furniture store, a fish-and-chips take-out place, and then, just past a drop-in medical clinic, he saw a plastic sidewalk sign, with hand-painted lettering reading

"The Bookstore of Other Languages." It seemed worth exploring. He opened the door, a chime rang, and he walked in.

Rows of bookshelves filled the room, cardboard sign hanging above them from the ceiling. Under Français he could see several shelves. It might be fun to try to read something simple. He could guess what language Dansk was, but what was Eesti? Estonian? Maybe. But 한국어? Or български език? Amazing! He had no idea this place was here.

Bryce's high school French and Spanish classes were twenty years behind him. He found the shelves under the Español sign and looked for a dictionary or a teach-yourself-Spanish book. That might be interesting. But there were none, just books, some new, some used, arranged by author. He was pleased to recognize Allende, Bolaño, Borges, and Cervantes, but there were dozens of others he'd never heard of. He reached for a book at random and opened *El Castillo Interior*, by Teresa de Ávila. The name sounded familiar, but he couldn't place her.

"Can I help you?" A small gray-haired woman with a pixie haircut was at his elbow, smiling. A golden sun hung from one ear and a silver moon from the other.

"Wow," he said. "I've never been in a bookstore like this. How many different languages do you have?"

"We only carry forty to fifty here in the shop, but we can get you others if you are interested."

"Who comes here? There can't be enough people around Seattle to, well, excuse me, but to keep you in business."

Her smile widened. "We just opened, but eventually people will come from all over the world."

Bryce's skepticism was apparent. "No," he said. "Not really."

"We are unique, you know," she said, still smiling. "What languages are you interested in?"

"I took French and Spanish in high school, but that was a long time ago."

"Well, if you could know any language, any language at all in the whole world, what would it be?"

Bryce thought about the classics he could read – Don Quixote, maybe, or something older. What if he could read Canterbury Tales in Middle English, or even Beowulf? But then, maybe he'd like to learn a language that would let him travel. Swedish, maybe, or Greek, or Japanese.

"It kind of depends," he said. "I don't know if I'd like to learn a language that would help me read books, or a language that would help me travel."

"If you decide to travel we have a tourist level, and it's probably a good place to start, and of course it comes with reading ability. Once you're comfortable with that, you can always choose a higher level of fluency."

"I'm completely lost. I have no idea what you're talking about."

The little gray-haired woman nodded. "You didn't know about us before? How is it that you've come here?"

"I always look for bookstores, but I don't understand what you're doing. Or if I do understand, it's not very believable."

She nodded again. "Why don't I get Cilla to start from the beginning and explain it to you? I'm Blythe. Your name?"

"Bryce. Bryce Hanford."

She looked over to a corner where a young woman was un-packing books.

"Cilla?"

The young woman looked up.

"Could you please tell Mr. Hanford about us?"

Cilla was so remarkably like a grown-up version of the little girl in the hospital cafeteria that Bryce was now sure that he had crossed over into some alternate universe. Perhaps his elation at being well, at not going to die after a period of un-bearable treatment, alone in a sterile and heartless hospital room, had led him into a hallucinatory state, where he was at-tended by smiling brown-skinned girls dressed in pale pink, their hair neatly braided in cornrows. A thin voice in a distant place in his mind said, "It's a coincidence! Coincidences hap-pen!" but the voice was too far away and the dizzy delight of the moment was irresistible.

"Are you okay?"

He stared at Cilla. "Oh. Sorry. Yes. Fine."

"I'm Cilla."

"Bryce Hanford."

"So, Bryce, how did you happen to come here today?"

Bryce wanted to tell her the whole story. At a quiet and el-egant restaurant. At home at the dinner table.

"Really, are you okay?"

"Yes! Yes. Okay. Well. Yes, I just was going for a walk and I happened to find you and it's a bookstore and I like books, es-pecially history, and I was curious, so I came in. Where am I? What do you do here? What's going on?"

Cilla led him to a table and chairs at the back of the store and gestured for him to sit down.

"We're the Bookstore of Other Languages," she began." We sell books in every language that books are printed in. We also sell the ability to read or speak those languages."

"You're a language school?"

"Not exactly. Our method is unique. It was developed by Dr. Daniel Milton, a brilliant neuropsychologist. We just opened a few weeks ago, after many years of development and clinical testing that established that the process is completely safe, with no side effects. You buy the ability to read or speak a language and pay depending on the level of fluency you want and how long you want to have that language."

"It can go away?"

"Exactly. So, if you want, say, two weeks of enough Italian to get around and shop and ask questions, that would be tourist level, at one price; a year of business level fluency would be different; a lifetime at the level of a native speaker would be something else entirely. The level of reading ability matches the ability to speak. It's simple, really. It works."

"Have you tried it?"

"I just got back from Belize and it was so meaningful to have had Kriol. I met and talked with people in a completely different way than if I had just relied on English."

"So, I have this . . . procedure . . . and then I go to Athens and speak Greek with anybody I meet? I order from menus, I read newspapers, I ask for directions when I'm lost? Just like that?"

"Yes!"

"How much would it cost, say, to be able to speak tourist-level Russian for a month?"

"There's an initial mapping fee of $450. Tourist level of any language is $300 a week."

"God. How much is a life-time at the native speaker level?"

"It's a deal. $100,000."

"I don't get it. If I have the fluency, how is it going to disappear? How can there be a time limit on it?"

"Have you ever heard of transcranial magnetic stimulation?"

"Uh, no."

"Dr. Milton's process is a refinement of TMS, transcranial magnetic stimulation. It's a simple, non-invasive out-patient procedure that we do in our clinic next door. It's used to create pathways in the brain to treat, for instance, stroke victims. It's used to treat depression, too. Dr. Milton's breakthrough has been to use magnetic stimulation to trace new neural pathways in the language centers of your brain. The first time takes a couple of hours because we have to map your language centers in detail, but after that, we can do it in half an hour. You tell us what language you want, and so on, and we program the transcranial stimulation to embed the language. Here's a brochure that tells more."

Bryce sat back in his chair, closed his eyes, and breathed deeply. Cilla watched him with some concern.

"Mr. Hanford? Do you need anything? Can I get you something? Do I need to call 911?"

Cilla went to the door. "Blythe, can you bring me a glass of water?"

Blythe hurried into the room with a glass of water, which she placed on the table next to Bryce. He sat up, grabbed the glass, and gulped the water.

"This makes no sense," he said. "This is nuts. I'm going crazy. I'm out of here."

He put his hand on the table and pushed himself to his feet, stumbled through the shelves of books and out on the sidewalk, slamming the door behind him. He stopped to look at the clinic next door, but it looked like a free clinic for street people. He turned uphill and walked toward the hotel. He wasn't well. He needed to lie down.

REPORT: HANFORD, BRYCE

PRIMARY CONTACT: CILLA M.

REASON FOR CONTACT AND PROGNOSIS FOR FUTURE ENGAGEMENT:

Mr. Hanford entered the BOOL by chance. He seemed to be in a state of heightened consciousness, exhibiting a lack of focus and sensitivity to new information. His physical and emotional condition at the time of contact seemed unstable, though, leaving us with little information about the likelihood of any future interest on his part. Prognosis for future engagement is uncertain.

Entering the hotel, Bryce was afraid to look at the desk clerk, afraid that she might turn out to be a smiling, brown-skinned, corn-rowed woman dressed in light pink, but no. It was a portly, white-haired man in a dark suit and white shirt.

Bryce leaned against the elevator wall, got off and went to his room, and sat on the bed. He took off his shoes, pulled back the covers and lay very still. What a day! He was well. He was healthy. He had some time. He was only thirty-eight for God's sake. He took a long, slow breath, puffed out his cheeks, and blew it out.

What a day of women! Dr. Branch, the little girl, and her mother. Blythe. Cilla. Too many women. He wanted to go home. Why had he spent all this money for a hotel room when he could have just gone back home? He picked up his phone to check for messages. There was a text from Hal, *"Hey, there! How did it go?"* *"OK, but weird. Wait for the story,"* he wrote back. There were e-mails from political groups asking for money and his college asking for money, and the bookstore – the good bookstore, the one back home – telling about upcoming author visits.

He was hungry. It was after five-thirty and he hadn't had lunch. He was starving! He had to get food. He sat up suddenly, then lay back down. He thought about Cilla. He wanted to go to dinner with Cilla, to meet her at the Pike Street Market and find the Basque place, or to meet her at the Angelico Bar at the Hotel Toscana. He could meet her at work and they could get fish and chips. But when he thought about where she worked, at the Bookstore of Other Languages, he had to close his eyes again and breathe more long slow breaths.

He reached for the room service menu. No. He'd already wasted enough money. Damn if he'd have a glorified meatball sandwich for $20 plus a tip. He sat up, put his shoes back on. He went to the mirror and slowly combed his hair and smoothed his mustache. He put on his parka and went back out into the strange world.

This time he went south instead of west, walking by skyscrapers rather than old brick buildings, with no graffiti in sight. This was where law firms and accountants and fancy corporations had offices. Where men wore ties and women wore high heels, where they knew exactly where they were going and were striding purposefully along the sidewalk.

Bryce had an early dinner at a Spanish restaurant and tried not to think about the foreign words on the menu, then spent the evening walking around Seattle. He visited a photography gallery, then went into a clothing store and tried on a pullover, but didn't like the way it seemed to emphasize his stomach. He went into a very normal bookstore and bought a very normal bestselling legal thriller. He went back to his hotel room. As he took off his parka, he noticed something in the pocket – the brochure from the Bookstore of Other Languages. He glanced at the picture of a handsome blond man, "Dr. Daniel Milton, Ph.D., University of Leiden," then crumpled up the brochure and tossed it into the wastebasket. He was in bed by eight o'clock and read the legal thriller until he fell asleep. The next morning he checked out of the hotel, got in his car, and drove in a pounding rain north to Anacortes and the ferries that would take him home.

CHAPTER TWO

After his return from Seattle, Bryce thought more about the pullover and decided that Dr. Valerie was right and that he needed to lose weight. He remembered her advice to increase exercise by ten percent and to decrease calories by ten percent, and it seemed not too drastic. He knew what foods to cut back on – it would actually feel good to put the brakes on the beers, and that meant fewer chips, less guacamole, so far, so good, although he gave himself a free pass for Fridays at the Crab Pot with the Study Group.

The next Friday, he told them about his trip to Seattle. They shook their heads about the Bookstore, dismissing it as one more scam to fleece the credulous. Bryce also consulted them about exercise, but they weren't helpful. Hal, short and whippet thin, was a runner, which somehow seemed to suit an algebra teacher. Ginnie did yoga three times a week at the Blue Heaven Consciousness Center. Ashley was a former runner who had given it up and accepted a fifteen-pound penalty.

"It's hard," said Ashley. "There is no commercial gym on the Island, and blech, who wants to go to a gym anyway?"

"I would," said Hal, "if they had weight training. But I probably wouldn't have the time. Evan has started soccer and I don't know how this happened, but all of a sudden I'm the coach."

"I would," said Ginnie, "if they had mixed martial arts. It would be a great corrective to all the high-minded people at yoga. I'd love to add some bash 'em up exercise. I figure I get my weight training at work, lifting yearbooks."

"But since you don't want to run," said Ashley, you don't want to do yoga, and there is no commercial gym . . ."

Hal and Ginnie shook their heads sadly.

"Looks like you're getting a stationary bike," Ashley continued. "I couldn't handle it myself. Too boring."

Ginnie tilted her head (it always looked tilted because one side of her head was shaved, so only the left side of her face was framed by one long silver-blonde curl) and stared at him.

"It's rude to stare, Ginnie," Bryce said. "What are you thinking?"

"It's not rude to stare questioningly but encouragingly at a friend," she replied.

"What is it?"

"That's my encouraging question. What is it? Are you ready" –she narrowed her eyes meaningfully – "to try again?"

"What I'm ready to do is lose some weight. I don't know about trying again. The truth, and I don't want to hear your opinion of it, is that I miss Sheila."

Ginnie sat up straight. "Let me ask you a question."

"No."

"Was Sheila ever happy? Was Sheila ever satisfied?"

"Shut up, Ginnie. And, no, not with me. But she was cool in other ways. Besides, am I happy? Am I ever satisfied?"

"Well, are you?"

"No."

They sat silently.

"The thing is, I don't have a clue why not."

His friends shook their heads.

"Sorry, Bryce, don't think we can help you with that," said Ashley.

Bryce took the car to the mainland, bought a stationary bike, brought it home and did a half hour morning and evening. In the mornings he listened to the news on the radio; in the evening he listened to audio books. He paid more attention to what and how much he was eating and lost some weight. He got a little fitter, and he found to his surprise, that the end result was not so much satisfaction as restlessness. With more energy came the discovery that he was bored. He wanted to get out a little. And maybe it was time to "try again," to meet some women.

When Bryce's phone played Merle Haggard singing "Mama Tried" it meant Linda was calling. When Linda called him at work, it meant trouble.

"What's up, Mom?"

"Oh, Bryce, I don't know what to do."

"Tell me what's going on."

"It's Brenda."

"Brenda who?"

"Your cousin, Brenda! Mel's daughter!"

"What's she done now?"

"She's disappeared."

"What?"

"Listen to me. Mel's here and he's falling apart with worry. Brenda is an attractive, single woman. She has no business hitch-hiking alone in Eastern Europe. And now it's been three weeks since Mel has heard from her."

"Mom, there's nothing wrong with a grown-up woman hitchhiking if she wants to. I'm sure Brenda is perfectly competent. Besides, Brenda is rich enough to buy her way out of anything. And besides that, Brenda hates me. I have not had one pleasant conversation with Brenda ever in my entire life. Even Stevie, the husband that was, was friendlier than Brenda, and Stevie can be pretty intimidating." He paused to take a breath. "What does Dad say?"

"Your father says the hell with her, but then he says he's worried, too. Listen - here's your uncle."

"Bryce!"

"Uncle Mel! What's going on?"

"Bryce, what do you think? I'm seventy-eight years old. You think I can stop my daughter from doing crazy things? No! But what can I do when she disappears?"

"Uncle Mel, maybe she's busy sight-seeing. I mean, seriously, I know you're worried, but have you had bad news? What have you heard?"

There was a silence. Bryce had the impression that Uncle Mel was crying.

"I'm telling you, Bryce, every Friday, every Friday without fail she sends me an e-mail, wherever she is. She started out in

Athens and wanted to hitchhike around the Adriatic. Every Friday she sent me an e-mail. Three and half weeks ago she sent me an e-mail from Corfu. She was going on to Albania. I haven't heard from her since. She could have been kidnapped."

"Uncle Mel, really I'm not trying to be funny, but who would they try to get money from? She's the only rich one in the family. They'd have to send the ransom notes about Brenda to Brenda. No, wait! Uncle Mel, have you got in touch with Stevie?"

"No! Why would I get in touch with him? They're divorced, why would I get in touch with Stevie? Besides, you can't just get in touch with Stevie. You have to call somebody who calls somebody else, who calls somebody else."

"I'm just thinking, if, just in case, if anybody did kidnap Brenda, they'd try to get money from Stevie. That was the divorce that made her so rich, and that was probably pocket change for Stevie."

"Think again, Bryce. Nobody in their right mind would mess with Stevie. Even if half the things they say about him are true, the kidnappers wouldn't dare. You don't think he made Brenda disappear?"

Bryce rolled his eyes. "No! If Stevie was going to make Brenda disappear he would have done it years ago. Listen. Call him anyway. He's not such a bad guy. I mean, yeah, he probably is, but he's always been reasonable with us. After all, he stepped in to protect Brenda a couple of years ago."

"That wasn't protecting Brenda – that was protecting Nina. Protecting an ex-wife is one thing; protecting a daughter is something else. Nobody wants to read in the paper that their mother was arrested for shoplifting."

"Uncle Mel – what do you have to lose? Call Stevie!"

"Okay, you're right, I'll call him. I'll try. Bryce, I'm so worried! And Albania!" Mel's voice rose. "Who knows anything about Albania? What will happen to her?"

A thumping noise and then silence. Bryce could hear the exchange of urgent voices.

"Bryce? It's Mom. Mel dropped the phone. Look – Mel says either you go or he goes. The flight leaves Seattle tomorrow night at 10:40. Mel will pay for everything – airfare, hotel, bribes, ransom, whatever you need. He'll overnight you his credit card."

"Okay, Mom. Tell Uncle Mel it's okay. I'll go. But tell him he has to call Stevie, just in case."

He hung up and stared at the phone. He looked over at his assistant, who was staring intently at a screen as if he were waiting for it to hatch.

"Justin?"

"Yeah?"

"How do you feel about running the shop for a week?"

Justin leaned back in his chair and opened his eyes wide. He took a deep breath and blew it out, making his round cheeks even rounder. "Wow. Sheesh. I don't know. What do I do if I have to make a service call?"

"Put a sign on the door, I guess."

Justin rubbed his fingers through his curly black hair. "Oh. Okay. Why not? Wow. A whole week?"

"I have never prayed so ardently. Please, please, God, make it be as short as possible."

"Where are you going?"

"Albania. That's why all the prayers. Not that I think God spends much time there."

"I didn't mean to eavesdrop, but this sounds kind of dramatic."

"When you're talking about Uncle Mel and Cousin Brenda, Drama R Us."

"I hate that."

"No shit. Justin, I have to take a walk."

"Got it. See you later."

Bryce went outside and walked to the end of the block. He pulled his phone out of his pocket and stared at it, then turned it on and searched the web for The Bookstore of Other Languages, found the number and called. Blythe answered and he made an appointment for the next day.

The next day, suitcase packed, and with Mel's credit card in his wallet, Bryce drove to Seattle. At the Bookstore, Cilla was waiting for him. She was so beautiful she seemed iridescent. Her eyes were huge, her eyelids were dusted with pale blue, her lips glistened. She was wearing a white lace blouse and a long white skirt and she seemed to shimmer.

"Hello, again," she said, "and welcome. Ready to start?"

"Yeah."

"You remember that the first time takes a while because we have to do the mapping, right?"

"A couple of hours, you said."

"Right. Then what? How would you like to start? Ready for a trip to Belize?"

"Well, we have a family emergency, so I don't really have a choice. I need Albanian for a week."

"What level? Travel, business, or native speaker?"

"Oh, business, I guess."

"It's $450 for the initial scan and then $500 for one week of Albanian at business level reading, writing, and speaking. Any other questions?"

"What happens at the end of the week? The language will just go away?"

"Right. I know, it's hard to believe, but for a week you'll be speaking Albanian and when the week is over it will go away. Anything else?"

"What do I have to do to speak Albanian? I mean, I get it that I'll be able to speak it, but do I just decide to speak it and then I speak it?"

"At first you'll find yourself responding unconsciously to external cues. With a little practice, you'll be aware of which language you're speaking and you'll be able to switch codes easily. It won't be a problem."

"Oh."

No other questions occurred to him. He handed Cilla Mel's credit card and she ran the transaction. He signed a boilerplate release form. She then led him to the clinic next door, the supposed free street clinic. Cilla smiled at the receptionist, who gave her a discreet nod and smile. Cilla turned in to a hallway and opened a door on the left, and there was Blythe in a lab coat standing next to what looked like a dentist's chair.

"Welcome!" she said. "Have a seat. Now, truly, this doesn't hurt at all – I've done it many times, but if you'd like a sedative?"

"No, I don't think so."

"The first time does take a while. You'll hear a kind of rat-a-tat noise, but you could listen to music as a distraction. What kind of music do you like?"

"Oh, I don't know. Classical? Something beautiful to take my mind off this?"

"Vocal? Instrumental?"

"Oh, you choose. I've got too much on my mind."

"Just relax in this chair, Mr. Hanford."

He sat back uneasily while Cilla adjusted monitors and positioned an instrument of some sort on his head and then headphones over that. His thumb began to twitch, and it reminded him somehow of Macbeth, but then he heard the welcome sound of an easy, unforced soprano gliding into the Songs of the Auvergne, and he let it go.

REPORT: INITIAL MAPPING AND TMS

HANFORD, BRYCE, CLIENT #0022

INITIAL SCAN: $450

LANGUAGE, LEVEL OF PROFICIENCY, DURATION, PRICE:

ALBANIAN, BUSINESS, ONE WEEK: $500

TECHNICIAN: CILLA M.

REASON FOR CONTACT AND PROGNOSIS FOR FUTURE ENGAGEMENT:

Mr. Hanford had a family emergency in Albania. He appears to have no lasting interest, at least at this point, in pursuing this language. He is, however, an intelligent man with an interest in history and other cultures. Regardless of the outcome of his family situation, he has now had the initial mapping and primary language programming. I assess his potential as a long-term BOOL client to be better than average.

That evening, exhausted and with the feeling that he might have a headache at any minute, Bryce drove to the airport and got on a plane bound for New York City. From there he flew to Rome, then Istanbul, and from there to the proudly contemporary Tirana International Airport Mother Theresa, where he arrived twenty-five hours after leaving Seattle. It was almost nine on a chilly, smoggy April morning. He looked through the glass walls to see palm trees surrounded by asphalt. He walked along with a loud quarreling family, exhausted parents holding sleepy tots and a group of excited students to passport control, where he showed his papers.

"Good morning!" The young woman in uniform behind the desk smiled at him. She had wide cheeks, thick blonde hair, and her smile was tired.

Grateful for any smile, Bryce forced a smile on his own lips. "Good morning."

The young woman, whose name was Afrodita according to her badge, examined his passport with a look of surprise.

"Are you here on business or for pleasure?"

"Oh, looking up family."

"Ah, that explains it," she said, and Bryce thought her smile might have widened a bit.

It all seemed a bit mysterious, but wanting to get to the end of the airport gauntlet, he smiled back, took his papers, picked up his backpack and moved to security. There, too, everything went smoothly, and he was soon free to choose from the enthusiastic taxi drivers, eager to take him to the Polaris Tirana Hotel, where he had optimistically reserved a two-bedroom suite.

After a terrifying cab ride through seemingly lawless streets, Bryce arrived at the hotel, inspected his suite, found nothing alarming, and decided that shaving came first, and then breakfast, with plenty of coffee. That accomplished, he approached the concierge.

"Good morning."

The concierge lifted his eyebrows. "Good morning, sir! Welcome to Tirana! How may I help you?"

"It's a little complicated," Bryce began, "I'm trying to find a lost relative." He described the situation and asked how to get in touch with hospitals and with the police. The concierge made helpful suggestions and gave Bryce the name of a lawyer, a Mr. Berisha.

After that, it wasn't so very hard. Mr. Berisha discovered that Brenda was not being held in any jails or prisons in the country, and meanwhile, Bryce made a list of local hospitals. He found her at the second stop. Yes, Mrs. Bongiorno was a patient at the hospital, and was he here to pay for her care?

It turned out that Brenda had stumbled in a hole in the sidewalk, breaking her nose, a few ribs, and a leg. Passersby had called for help, but not before a more enterprising passerby had made off with Brenda's backpack and wallet. She had her passport, but no way to pay her hospital bill. Bryce flourished Uncle Mel's credit card and was soon directed to Brenda's room.

He found Brenda with one leg was in a cast; a white shield-like bandage covered her nose.

"Hi," he said. "I'm your cousin, Bryce. I'm here to help."

Brenda glared at him from blackened eyes.

"Took you long enough."

After being informed by the doctor that Brenda was recovering satisfactorily and would be released in a few days, Bryce found that he had time to see the sights in Tirana. First, though, he thought he would sleep, and he did. He hung the Do Not Disturb sign on his door and slept for twelve hours. He then took a long shower and dressed slowly, enjoying the sense of having no responsibilities and no sense of urgency. Downstairs in the lounge, he had an ample and leisurely breakfast, lingering over the sweet raisin pilaf, feta cheese baked in filo pastry, thick yoghurt, and coffee.

He strolled out the door into a gentle spring day and decided to follow his nose. After stubbing his toe on an uneven sidewalk and remembering Brenda, he walked carefully through the crowded streets, full of loud vendors, people talking into cell phones, shoppers with colorful bags, and dawdling tourists. He went into a bookstore and bought a history of Albania. In Skanderbeg Square, he found a splendid mosque and several museums. Choosing the National History Museum, he wandered through its many pavilions in three stories of exhibits, looking over everything from ancient artifacts to relics of life behind the Iron Curtain, including Albania's brutal labor camps. By the time he was finished it was time for a late lunch, and after a comfortable meal of fish and pasta, salad and wine, Bryce felt up to calling on Brenda.

Her white nose shield was gone, revealing two bloodshot eyes surrounded by purple circles that were surrounded by yellow circles.

"Where have you been?" she croaked. "Do you have a pen and paper?"

"Right here," he answered. "I wanted to ask you what I might pick up for you."

"Make a list. Volumizing shampoo. But not anything perfumey. If you can't get fragrance free, then get something citrusy. But if you can't get that then go to another store. Conditioner. Unscented only. Or citrus, but only if you can't find unscented."

The list went on, through deodorants, facial soaps and moisturizers, vitamins and various supplements, and then went on to clothes, including underwear, a wide skirt, and a shirt that buttoned in the front. She'd need shoes, but she'd only need the left shoe since her right leg was in a cast, but she'd need orthotics. Later he could take her to stores and she could pick out what she wanted to wear until she got home. Also a plane ticket back to Seattle with him. He could pick her up on Monday afternoon and take her back to the hotel. On Tuesday they would go shopping and the next day fly out. He would have to get her a first-class seat that would accommodate her leg. Also, she wanted gluten-free snacks and meals from each of the airlines.

Bryce found that his one day of leisure was his last and that afterward the time passed painfully. After much searching in stores, he was able to assemble a close approximation of Brenda's requirements, although not to her satisfaction; after much arguing and pleading with airlines he was allowed to spend Uncle Mel's money to provide Brenda with most of her desired circumstances.

Brenda was released from the hospital on Monday and moved into the hotel with Bryce, where she determined that he had taken the better bedroom. Sheets were changed, drugs were taken, the door was closed, and she was blessedly quiet for the rest of the evening. After spending the next day pushing her in her wheelchair to various boutiques, then accompanying her to the hotel's beauty salon, Bryce was more than ready to go home.

It was late afternoon when they arrived at the airport. Bryce maneuvered his freshly coiffed and manicured cousin and her tiger-print luggage through various gates and through security. He explained the situation to the agent at the boarding gate, a pleasant young woman who helped them negotiate the last few yards to the door of the plane, where she smiled at them, waved, and said: "Udhëtim i sigurt!"

"What?" he said. But she had turned was walking back up the ramp.

On the plane to Istanbul, Brenda snapped at the flight attendant, demanding extra snacks and single-malt whiskey. After taking a greedy gulp, she turned and looked at Bryce sourly. "You were speaking Albanian," she said.

Bryce immediately and unreasonably felt defensive about the Bookstore. "As you already know," he replied, "the trip from Seattle to Tirana takes twenty-five hours. I spent most of it memorizing *One Hundred Phrases for Doing Business in Albania.*"

"Where is it now?"

"What?"

"The book, pamphlet, the *One Hundred Phrases*?"

"I left it at the hotel."

"I never saw it."

"You never looked beyond your own needs."

"Why did you leave it?"

He looked her firmly in the eye. "Because I will never again use it in my life. Believe me."

"You never stopped to think that I might be able to use it." She picked up the history of Albania that was on his tray. "You bought this. You going to read this book?"

He opened it and realized that it was written in Albanian. "It's just a souvenir. I can't read a word of it."

CHAPTER THREE

E-mail from Marina to Astrid:

As you know, even though I travel all over, I remain a loyal citizen of France. I just want to say, though, and with no disrespect to my country, that Charles de Gaulle is the MOST HORRIBLE FUCKING AIRPORT IN ALL THE WORLD. Unlike many others, though, they do have Ladurée stands and I'm sweetening myself up first with one pistachio macaron and then an Earl Grey, then a pistachio, then an Earl Grey. And so the sweetening process continues.

Thank you again for the use of your convenient Paris apartment! Which I left in perfect order as always (except that one time, but you've forgotten about that, right?) I'm off to the San Juan Islands, which you would think would be in some Spanish part of the world, but are far off in the northwest of the United States. Seattle is the nearest big city, or maybe Vancouver. There's something very attractive to me in the idea of an island, but I'm not sure what. Maybe because they're almost sure to have beaches. We'll see how Eliza Island compares to Rhodes.

Kiss Thérèse for me. I hope she's over her cold. I know it's an impossible thing to wish for, but your mother should stop smoking. She would feel better. And many kisses to you!
Marina

Back home, Bryce felt like he never wanted to leave again. Adventures were altogether too wearing, and worn out was what he was. No more. No more travel, no more drama, and most of all no more Brenda. He had delivered her to her father and felt that he had paid up any family obligations far into the future.

Justin had done very well. He'd sold devices, installed networks, scrubbed out malware, even satisfied their one permanently dissatisfied customer, negotiating a decent compromise. Too bad, thought Bryce, that he would never leave the store to Justin again because he had no intention of ever leaving the island again. He gave Justin a raise, a new title, and new business cards. He was happy to go back to work, and to daily life. He came home from work in the lengthening days and worked on projects, surrounding his raised garden beds with a deer-proof fence and building a deck on the back of the house. In the evenings he read about revolutions – he moved from France to Russia, then back to the New World to Mexico. He limited travel to reading and to imaginary trips taken on his stationary bike.

Life went on quietly on the Island, with small changes. June came and school was over. Curtis sold the bicycle shop and retired, happy to be able to leave the shop and go on his own rides. The physical therapy clinic next door to the Eliza Island Medical Center got a new massage therapist, and Dr. Valerie introduced Bryce to her, a Marina Ollivier. Marina was as tall as Bryce and as fit as Valerie, with long, straight, silky black hair and the bluest eyes that Bryce had ever seen. She was French, from Brittany. On an impulse, he asked her out to lunch and she accepted.

Over fajitas at Lo Tengo, they traded bits of information about themselves.

Marina got right to the point. "So, here we are," she said. "Tell me your life."

"Oh, grew up in Portland, Oregon, went to Portland State, didn't know what I wanted to study. I mean, what I really liked was history. My dad taught high school history – but I didn't want to teach and I knew I was going to need to make a living, so I studied computer science. The problem was that I never really committed to either history or computer science. I wasn't like the crazy guys who ate code for breakfast, and I didn't qualify for the kind of jobs they got, either. I knew enough to go to work for a company that installed networks for businesses, and then I found out about this business here that was for sale and I bought it. Married, divorced, that's it. Well, and I love it here – it's beautiful, I like the people, the business is doing okay."

He shrugged and smiled at her. "Counting my blessings. Your turn. What brought you to the States?"

"Okay. After university, I didn't know what to do. I wanted to travel, so I went to Florida and studied massage therapy. I can always find a job, especially in places where there are rich tourists who need massages, so I go all over."

Her voice was the smoothest alto speaking voice that he had ever heard, swooping and gliding over her sentences. It wasn't only the blackness of her hair, he thought, but the way the fine black strands floated around her smiling face.

Bryce became aware that he was staring at her. He looked down into his salad and speared a piece of tomato. "Where else have you traveled?"

"I hitchhiked all through Spain and Portugal one year, but then I decided that I wanted to visit as many islands as possible. I spent a summer in Ireland. It was so beautiful, but not so much to my taste when it got darker in the fall, so I went off to Greece and stayed in Rhodes for a while, then Majorca. Bali is incredibly beautiful. Martinique. I suppose that now that I'm thirty I should settle down, but I'm not ready. I'm enjoying myself too much. How about you? Do you travel?"

"I go nowhere," Bryce said, feeling slightly pitiful. It suddenly occurred to him then that he had traveled just this year. "That's actually not entirely true; I did make a trip earlier this year to Albania."

Marina lifted her black eyebrows and widened her blue eyes. "That's different. Why were you interested in Albania?"

"Not so interested - I was getting my cousin out of a jam. She was hitchhiking, too, but ran into some trouble and I had to come to the rescue."

"So it was a family adventure?"

He sipped his coffee. "Not much of an adventure, just mostly a pain in the butt." He changed the subject. "Your English is great – you learned it in school?"

"Of course. All French kids study English. Then wherever I travel I wind up using English. I don't suppose you studied Albanian."

"Well, I picked up a little when I was there, but I've forgotten it all now. It really wasn't a great trip."

Marina shrugged and her hair moved around her face. "Sounds like you need to take another trip to clear the palate."

He thought for a minute, then smiled at her. "Where do you think I should go?"

She shrugged. "I don't know – where would you like to go?"

"That's the thing. I don't know. I'm pretty flexible. I could go hiking or on a walking trip, but I could go to bookstores and restaurants and museums and concerts. I could walk around and look at neighborhoods, or I could just sit in a park and watch the world go by. Probably wherever I'd go I'd be interested in the history of the place. History is kind of my lost love, wherever I find it – here or really anywhere. I've been reading about revolutions recently."

He paused and thought again, then looked into her eyes. "You know, I just realized something. I wonder if I'm reading about revolutions because I need one myself."

Marina smiled. "You should do like everybody else, then. Go to Paris."

"Really? Everybody says it's expensive and they hate us."

"Pfft!" She thought for a minute then smiled at him. "Tell me - do you have summer tourists here in the San Juans?"

"Are you kidding? They crowd into the ferries, they're loud, they drive up the cost of everything, they act like we're here to fill their every need, they wander around clueless like they're stoned not paying attention to where they're going, and generally mess up everything. The only good thing they do here is spend money. Hardly worth it if you ask me."

Marina looked at him inquiringly.

"Oh," he said. "Well, if you put it that way."

"You know what?" She smiled teasingly. "Paris has a history. Not to mention a revolution."

Bryce smiled back.

Carlos came by to see if they wanted dessert. They decided that they didn't, and Bryce asked for the check. Behind Marina's back, Carlos caught Bryce's eye, glanced at Marina, and made an approving gesture. Out on the sidewalk, Bryce and Marina parted to go back to their work.

E-mail from Astrid to Marina:

By now you're half-way around the world, but then, what do I expect? Is it as beautiful as you thought? Send me pictures! I do wonder what the attraction is of an island. There is a romance about them somehow. I wouldn't mind seeing Martinique. Did you know that that was where Empress Josephine grew up?

Mama is much better, thanks. I think mostly she's bored. It is such a sad thing to be widowed for so long, and too bad that she didn't marry again. She would love to have someone to flirt with and to argue with. Alas, there is no one at the moment to flirt with, and I have gotten very good about slipping away from arguments, so all she has left is cigarettes and the neighbors. She enjoys visiting the rental apartment when we go to clean it and do the laundry, and hopes every time that she can come across Mme.

Mercier. After every one of their arguments, they each look so live-ly.

I have more final exams to grade, and so far I have several slothful students who are going to be unpleasantly surprised at the results.

Love,

Astrid

By August Bryce was deliriously in love with Marina, in September and October they were together whenever they could be. They rented bicycles and rode across the island to the harbor where the yacht club's restaurant was open to the public. They walked along the coast, and Bryce taught her the names of the shorebirds. They rented a small sailboat and circumnavigated the island in one long warm sunny day, Marina spectacular in her bikini, Bryce in new swimming trunks, two sizes smaller. They took the ferry to another island and went to a dance, where Marina danced with abandon and didn't make fun of his dancing. In November it was over.

"You know," Marina explained with a smile and a shrug, "I always move on when winter comes. The sun is setting at 5:30 here and it's getting darker every day. It's spring in Australia. I know it's not really an island, but I'm giving it a chance."

"I guess I knew, but I'm stunned anyway."

"What can I say? Life is change. Especially for me. I haven't forgotten about your travels, though. You should go to Paris. My aunt has an apartment that she rents to friends. It would make your trip much more affordable. Her name is Astrid Ollivier and I've told her about you. Here's her e-mail."

She gave him a card with an e-mail address scribbled on it, kissed him, and was gone.

E-mail from Marina to Astrid:

I'm off again. I'm going to an almost island, Australia, not sure where. I hear the beaches around Adelaide are beautiful, but I'll start at Sydney and look around.

I've been seeing a very nice man named Bryce, and he seemed a little stupefied when I told him I was off to Oz, but I'm sure he'll get over it. He did get to know me, after all.

Now you must listen to me. Bryce really is very nice and I think you would like him. I have given him your e-mail and encouraged him to rent the apartment. I think you should give yourself a break, damn it, and go out with him! You'd like him, he likes to sit around and talk like you do. You don't have to fall in love, but won't you please just give yourself a chance? If he does come to Paris and if he rents the apartment you really ought to be grateful to me, but I hope you'll wind up being even more grateful.

Much love,

Marina

E-mail from Astrid to Marina:

Marina, you must stop. I'm serious. Don't do this again.

Astrid.

Bryce was as dazed by Marina's sudden absence as he had been by her sudden presence. He spent Thanksgiving with Hal and his family, and afterward, he and Justin began the busy holiday season. Half of their customers seemed to be nervous parents who felt that games had never been this expensive in their childhood and that it was wrong that they cost so much now; the other half were adoring grandparents eager to indulge their budding tech-genius grandchildren. At Christmas, Bryce drove down to Portland, enjoyed the time with his parents, his sister and her husband, and even Uncle Mel. Brenda was, as usual, absent, another cause for rejoicing.

In January, Bryce felt as if he had suddenly woken up. It was time to shake things up, he told himself sternly, but was unsure which things needed to be shaken. In the end, he thought why not take Marina's advice and go to Paris? He e-mailed Astrid Ollivier and arranged to rent her apartment for three weeks, and then, a year after his first visit to The Bookstore of Other Languages, he called and made an appointment.

Bryce had imagined that by now the Bookstore would be building on its successes, but it looked no different than when he first visited it. The hand-painted sidewalk sign was splattered with mud; the windows needed washing, the books were stacked haphazardly on dusty shelves.

Bryce had made up his mind that this time he would ask Cilla out to lunch, but when he arrived, she wasn't there, only a blond man in his forties, dressed in black slacks, a tight black t-shirt, and a leather jacket. Bryce felt as if he should recognize him, but all he could think was that he looked like Brad Pitt.

"May I help you?"

"Does Cilla still work here?" Bryce asked.

"Oh, yes, but not today. Was there something special she was going to help you with?"

"Yes. Well, I have an appointment."

"Ah. Well, I'm Dr. Daniel Milton. You are?"

"Bryce Hanford."

Milton smiled engagingly and reached out an arm for a manly handshake. "It's a pleasure, Bryce. Is this your first appointment?"

"No, but last time it was a family emergency. This is just a vacation."

"Well, whatever the occasion, Bryce, we're pleased to help make it the best possible experience. Blythe? Can you help Mr. Hanford?"

Blythe came out of the room at the side, looked at Bryce and smiled. "Oh, hello!" She nodded at Dr. Milton. He turned and went into an office at the back of the store.

"Hello, Mr. Hanford. I remember you! You went to Slovenia? No, Albania. How was it?"

"The language was the best part of the trip."

"I'm glad to know we helped. How can I help you today?"

"I have an appointment, but I'm not sure what I want, what level I want to be at, tourist or business. What do I get at the tourist level? Can I read books? Newspapers? Can I order in restaurants? Will I have a good accent or will I sound schoolboyish? When I was in Albania I had to talk with official types and argue with hospital administrators and employ a lawyer, so I needed business level. I don't plan on doing any of that in Paris, but I don't want to sound like I just took a class on French for tourists."

Blythe tilted her head to regard him and he saw that she was wearing her sun and moon earrings.

"You'll be fine with tourist level, I think. The reading level is daily newspapers and best sellers; the comprehension is television news; the vocabulary includes current slang and internet abbreviations. The grammar is pretty basic – you won't be getting the imperfect subjunctive, but you won't need it. Whatever level you choose, you always get good pronunciation. "

"Okay, then. I want three weeks of tourist-level French."

"Of course, you've already done the mapping."

"Right."

"That will be $900."

Blythe consulted a computer. "I see you've arrived in good time for your appointment. Ready?"

He pulled out his credit card, signed the release form, and that was that. They went into the treatment room and as Bryce picked out a music CD and sat back in the chair. Blythe adjusted the equipment and put on the headphones. Listening to a Bach cello suite, Bryce tried to relax. He found himself thinking about the brochure that Cilla had given him at his first light-headed visit to the Bookstore. There had been a picture of the handsome Dr. Milton on the brochure. That's where Bryce had seen him before. He was from somewhere . . . but then the treatment its little tapping sounds. He listened to the cello and his mind went elsewhere.

REPORT: TRANSCRANIAL MAGNETIC STIMULATION

HANFORD, BRYCE, CLIENT #0022

LANGUAGE, LEVEL OF PROFICIENCY, DURATION, PRICE:

FRENCH, TOURIST, THREE WEEKS: $900

TECHNICIAN: BLYTHE P.

REASON FOR CONTACT AND PROGNOSIS FOR FUTURE
ENGAGEMENT:

*This is Mr. Hanford's second session, and he seemed much
more relaxed. Last time was a family emergency, but this time he
says he is traveling only as a tourist. Excellent prognosis for future
engagement.*

Bryce arrived at Charles de Gaulle airport the next morning
and eventually emerged from the Denfert-Rochereau Métro
station to find overcast skies and streets full of wet, lumpy
snow. He consulted his instructions again, and headed down
the street, pulling his suitcase behind him. He passed by shops,
then stopped to look at the apartments above the shops across
the street, each with double glass doors opening to tiny
wrought-iron balconies flanked by shutters. He turned down a
cobblestoned side street, passed a hairdresser and a laundry.
At the music shop, he identified himself to Madame Fournier
and was given the keys to the street door and the apartment.
Climbing to the third floor, he found his apartment, let himself
in, and looked around. The tiny apartment had been set up for
rental, but whoever had done it had also made it their own.

Before he unpacked, Bryce went to the tall bookshelf.
There was a shelf of guidebooks, of course, but there were
other books as well – the stories of Maupassant in French, a
history of the city of Paris in English, novels by Patrick Modia-
no, France's recent Nobel-winner, more fiction and more
history. Colorful quilts lay on the sofa bed, and Bryce wondered if they were African. A framed poster of a Bonnard

exhibition hung on the wall. And taking up precious space was a large ficus in an Italian ceramic pot. *Why only three weeks?* he thought. *Why not three months?*

Astrid Ollivier had sent him pages of careful instructions. She told him exactly how to get to the apartment from the airport. She told him how to use lights, heat, water, laundry, and wi-fi. She added a local map of the quiet neighborhood in the Fourteenth District, marking the best shops for both general and special needs, such as cheese and wine. She noted emergency services, best Métro lines to tourist destinations, and finished up with observations and comments about the neighbors. Bryce hoped to meet M. André, his neighbor on the third floor; he hoped to avoid Mme. Mercier on the floor below. He unpacked, looked at the bed, and decided to tough it out until nighttime.

Without any plan, Bryce set out on foot to explore the neighborhood and beyond. He passed restaurants, shops, and offices, crossed busy intersections, and eventually arrived at an immense cemetery, unlike any he'd ever seen. He expected to see wide flat lawns and small rectangles of stone but the Montparnasse cemetery was a great icy metropolis of the dead. The monuments lined the paths like tall buildings on city streets; the paths stretched over acres in a regular grid. He paused at the graves of Jean-Paul Sartre and Simone de Beauvoir, where someone – a tourist? – had left a bouquet of pine branches and rose hips in the snow. He found a Jewish section and wondered at how the memorials to Cohens and Levys and Goldbergs had survived the Nazi occupation. He found several Dreyfus families, but not the Dreyfus, the army captain falsely accused of treason, whose trials electrified and divided the nation at the turn of the twentieth century.

Afterward, he was pleased to be able to sit quietly in a bar, reading the newspaper. He shopped for bread and cheese, salami and apples, tea and wine, speaking French easily, not worrying about the language. He walked back to the apartment. Back, he found himself thinking, home. He ate his simple dinner, pulled out the bed and made it with fresh sheets that had been left for him, got inside, pulled up the quilts, and slept.

The next day Bryce set off to walk, aiming vaguely for the river. He eventually found himself the Fifth District, and there, among coffeehouses and boutiques, he discovered the Musée Cluny, the medieval museum of Paris. He bought his ticket and went in. He took his time inspecting dragons carved in stone, stained glass partridges foraging in the grass, and a daintily ornamented manuscript filled with an improbably regular hand-written text. At last, he arrived at the famous Lady and Unicorn tapestries, a grand tribute to the senses, to the various forms of information and pleasure that the body gives the spirit.

He took his time following the lady from one sense to the next, each with its own magnificent tapestry. Accompanied by her lion and unicorn, parakeet or monkey, the lady tasted, listened, smelled, touched, and looked. She stood elegantly on hundreds of meticulously woven flowers as she played her portable organ; sat gracefully as she held up a mirror for the unicorn to regard his reflected image. The last tapestry was the largest and the most famous because it's not clear which of her senses is pictured. She looks out from the entry of a tent under the motto *À mon seul desir*. Bryce realized that only in this tapestry was she smiling, although cautiously. She held a necklace; an attendant held an open chest. Was she taking the necklace out of the chest, or putting it away? Was her guarded smile a reaction to the necklace itself or to her renunciation of it? Bryce stood and stared. He wanted to ask her what her sole desire was; ask her how anyone could have just one sole desire.

Back in the busy university district, he found bookstores and bought books on medieval iconography, on Paris in the Middle Ages, and on the Hundred Years' War. He bought a touristy tote bag. He made his way back slowly, stopping to look at window displays of hip eyeglass frames, shoes and handbags, and perfumes. He amused himself by going into a toy store and choosing gifts for his nephews. He stopped for coffee and pastry, examined his new books, and then made his way back to the apartment. In between the second and third floors, he met a man coming downstairs, bundled up to go out.

A big baritone voice boomed from the small elderly man, "Ah, what a pleasure!" he said, reaching his hand out. "Mme. Ollivier told me you would be here! I'm Phillipe André! Welcome to Paris! Want to come have a coffee with me?"

Bryce shook his hand and thanked him, grateful for the welcome, but explained that he had just had coffee and was tired from spending all day on his feet. With hearty expectations of another opportunity in the near future, M. André proceeded down the stairs. Bryce unpacked his purchases, poured himself a glass of wine, opened his tablet, and sat down to write an account of his day to the Friday Study Group.

The next day Bryce walked in the same direction through the previous night's fresh snow, past the Sorbonne, and over a bridge to Notre Dame Cathedral. Each exterior architectural detail was highlighted with snow, and under the gray sky, it looked insubstantial, like an immense white drawing projected into space. He went in and was struck by the curse of anticipation. He felt nothing. He hardly knew what he had been expecting, but whatever it was, he didn't find it in this frigid alien structure. He could imagine space explorers finding it in a remote and abandoned corner of the galaxy, a relic of a lost civilization.

He went out, unreasonably disappointed, and walked on without purpose, heading vaguely northwards. He thought about the city itself, how it continually adapted to changing times and technologies. When it was time to plumb buildings, Paris didn't tear down the building to make way for something new; it just plumbed the building. It had no apparent problem with adding electrical wiring to buildings that were hundreds of years old. They must have added the internet without so much as a Parisian shrug. Smiling suddenly, Bryce thought of the little summer cabin on Eliza Island that had grown into his home. On a much smaller scale, it had been transformed over its eighty or a hundred years in the same incremental way as this great city had for more than two thousand years.

He eventually came to the forbidding seventeenth-century façade of a building that had been wrenched into the twentieth century when it had become the Musée Picasso. Picasso had never interested him much, but why not give him a chance? Bryce thought. He was first struck by the improbable pairing of the elaborately ornamented building and the aggressively modern art, the art that seemed to kick history into the street. As he walked through galleries, slowing to look more carefully, it occurred to him that Picasso's art had itself become history.

He looked at Picasso's work again and began to think that he could see a little history in each of them. He needed a book about Picasso. He needed to come back. He headed for the bookstore, where he found books for himself and a t-shirt for his father.

He did come back, spending all the next day in the Picasso museum, sitting just as long in some of the rooms as he had sat with the unicorn tapestries. The sculptures showed how Picasso grabbed and used whatever material he wanted – stone, plaster, clay, wire, metal scraps from a workshop, a kitchen colander. Bryce saw more and more how the artist had done the same with style. When he wanted to draw on classical Greek art or African art, he did. When he wanted something new, he invented Cubism; he pretty much invented modern collage. He boldly took what he wanted. It seemed also to be his approach to women, too. Bryce found himself particularly drawn to the fierce and sad portraits of Jacqueline Roque, Picasso's second wife, and ultimately, his widow. Bryce knew nothing about her, had never heard of her.

He went back to the apartment and looked at the shelf of books he had accumulated. How would he get them home? He put water on to boil, then opened his new biography of Picasso, and looked up Jacqueline in the index, and began to read. Picasso was rich and famous when he courted her, but oh, he was old. He was seventy-two; she was twenty-six. Did she count on his living another eleven years? While he made four hundred portraits of her? The water boiled and Bryce made himself a pot of tea.

Someone knocked on the door. Could it be the amiable M. André? Or was it the cranky Mme. Mercier? Bryce went to the door, opened it, and at first thought that it was Jacqueline come to life. The woman had Jacqueline's dark, arched eyebrows, her high cheekbones, her straight nose, her dark hair. Looking neither fierce nor sad, she smiled inquiringly at him.

"Hello. Are you Bryce Hanford? I'm Astrid Ollivier."

He had no words.

"Is it Bryce? Yes?"

"Sorry! Yes, yes, it's Bryce. You just surprised me, that's all."

He stared at her, then caught himself.

"Hello. Please come in."

"Thank you," she said, dusted the snow off her hat, came in, and hung her hat and coat on the rack in the hall, next to Bryce's parka.

"I have a fresh pot of tea. Would you like some?"

"Thank you, yes."

"I guess I'm a little confused," he said. "Do you live here? Do you need to move in? Is anything wrong?"

"No, no. I just came by to see how you were doing." There was music in her voice.

Bryce poured her tea. "So, this is not your home?"

She smiled and shook her head. Bryce saw that unlike Jacqueline's, Astrid's eyes were blue.

"Marina didn't explain the details, I see. I live with my mother, who is mostly lovely, but sometimes a little difficult and complains that she is in poor health. Mostly I think she is very bored. And she smokes too much and then she catches a cold. So I have this apartment as a retreat when I need it, and rent it out at other times, so it pays for itself."

"Oh." He stared at her.

Now she openly laughed.

"By any chance at all," she asked, "is it possible that you have been visiting the Musée Picasso?"

"Oh, my God!" he said. "Everybody does this, right?"

"I am famous among my friends for my resemblance to Jacqueline. You should see me at a costume party, made up as a Picasso painting."

He took a deep breath and sighed. "I guess I don't feel quite so foolish. And I have to add that your voice is remarkably like Marina's."

"Everyone in the family says that it's my grandmother's – Marina's great-grandmother's – voice."

Astrid took her cup and walked over to the table, where Bryce's newly-acquired library lay in stacks. She picked one up.

"Oh, this is a very good account of the Vichy time. How did you know about it? Was it reviewed in America?"

"Just got lucky, I guess. I browse in bookstores and buy too much and now I don't know how I'm going to get it all home. You 're interested in history?"

"It's what I do. I teach history and geography at a lycée a few blocks away."

"I want to talk with you! I want to know so much, and especially about the buildings. I suppose architecture is the proper word, but just the ordinary buildings are so interesting."

She nodded.

He went on. "I had this epiphany of sorts. I've been so struck by all the old buildings that have been used over time, not torn down whenever some developer got an idea for how to make another buck."

Astrid nodded. "Well, much of Paris, yes, but then there was Haussmann."

"Never heard of him."

"He ran a kind of urban renewal project in the mid-nineteenth century and demolished and rebuilt much of the city. We still don't have a consensus about his work. It's true that he got rid of dreadfully unsanitary buildings. It's also true that he forced thousands of poor people out of their homes."

"Could we go out and I could buy you a drink? I bet you know a good place in the neighborhood."

Astrid took him to a neighborhood bar in the next block, where they sat in a quiet booth next to the window. It was late afternoon, getting dark, and people were on their way home from work. It was pleasant to sit and watch people walk by, some of them carrying bags of groceries, others holding their children's hands. It was pleasant, too, to sit and look at Astrid. He began to see not only Jacqueline but also Marina. Astrid's hair was shorter than Marina's but its black silky waves made the same aura around her face. He forced himself to pay attention.

"Tell me about your interests in history," he said. You have a master's degree? A Ph.D.?"

"I have a master's degree in history, specializing in World War I, more broadly, from the Franco-Prussian War and the unification of Germany to the economic collapse of 1929. I wrote my thesis on the Dreyfus affair and the intersection of anti-Semitism and anti-feminism. You know, women did not vote in France until 1945."

"Here I thought France was so sophisticated."

"Ha! You are so wrong! The United States was thirty years ahead of us. At least you are ahead of us in that respect. But I've always suspected that women's suffrage in America might owe something to the women who settled the West. Wyoming was the first state to give women the vote, or at least that's what you usually hear. You know, in the early years of the Republic, some women had the vote and then it was taken away."

"Of the French Republic?"

"No, no – of your Republic."

"No!"

"Oh, yes. In the late eighteenth century, in several of the U.S. states women with property voted, and then, one by one, the states took the vote away from them."

"I never heard that."

"Ah, well, but it is true nonetheless."

Bryce drank the last of his beer. "Want another?"

"No, thanks."

Bryce ordered another beer for himself. "Tell me about your degree. Where did you study? What is your degree called? How does it work?"

She explained the French post-graduate system, then asked, "How is it that you speak French so well, but don't know about such things? Are your parents French?"

"Uh, well. It's a little complicated. I studied with a very effective system."

She lifted her eyebrows. "It seems that you're not eager to explain."

"No, it's still in the experimental stages. How about dinner?"

She took him to a place that wasn't on his list of online recommendations, a Breton restaurant, where the staff knew Astrid well and greeted her warmly. Over sausage crêpes, she explained that the owner was her cousin Hervé.

"Speaking of family," he said, "how is it that you are Marina's aunt, but seem to be her age. Is it that French women don't age like the rest of us do?"

"No, I assure you, we do get old, just like everybody else, although the difference may be that we don't apologize for it. My mother, for example, is sixty and will never give up. The answer to the riddle is that Marina's grandfather is my father. He married twice. She is the granddaughter from the first marriage and I am the daughter from his late second marriage. It's my mother whose life is like Jacqueline's; she was twenty-two when she married my father, and he was fifty-two. So she has had a long widowhood. But it was my mother's mother who looked like Jacqueline. So I am Marina's aunt, but only five years older. "

"I see. Mostly. I think I'd need to see a diagram."

"But how about you and Marina? Do you want to tell me about it?"

"Not really. She's beautiful, she lights up the room, she lights up my heart, and then she leaves. That's the story."

"I love her, you know. But it sounds as if you got to know the Marina that others have gotten to know."

Bryce was silent. Astrid looked at him and it seemed to him that she was gently holding him under a magnifying glass.

"You don't want to talk about Marina and you don't want to talk about your language studies. I'm afraid, Mr. Hanford, that if we share a meal you will have to tell me something about yourself."

Bryce felt as if he had been trapped by a naturalist, someone who wished him no ill but wanted, all the same, to observe and examine his behavior. He told her about his aimless education and its practical conclusion. He told her about life on an island in the Salish Sea, so far from Paris. He told her about his restlessness, his curiosity about the world, his inability to direct that restlessness and curiosity. Astrid listened without comment, only adding a question when he stopped talking. By the time they were finished, he felt as if he had told the story of his life not to Astrid, but to himself, and could now see and think about it in a different light.

She broke the silence. "Thank you for dinner. Please let me know if there's anything you need while you're here."

"Will I see you again?"

"What do you have in mind?"

He jumped at the opportunity. "A tour. I want a tour of Belle Époque Paris or World War I Paris or Haussmann's Paris, or of Gertrude Stein's Paris, or any Paris you want to show me."

"You're living in her old neighborhood, you know."

"Gertrude's? Really? Seriously, won't you just take me for a walk one day? Tell me what to read up on and I'll do it."

"All right. Sunday afternoon?"

"Yes! What shall I read?"

"Just look around in the books you already have. We'll start with the Lost Generation, the time when young Americans came to Paris to paint and write before they got famous. But then we'll probably digress. When you're a scholar you can't digress, but when you're a tourist – well, digression is one of the pleasures and liberties. When we've taken the walk you'll have a better sense of what you might want to read."

Outside the restaurant, she offered a hand, and he shook it. She put on her hat and walked down the block, and Bryce thought about how many hours it was until Sunday afternoon and he could indulge in digression with Astrid.

E-mail from Astrid to Marina:

Oh, you are bad. Bryce is here and I think you are crazy to have left him, but then I think again, and I know he's not for you now. You still need an adventurer, someone active and full of energy and ready to go! But then I think again and I realize that an adventurer would be so much fun for you, but that you don't need anyone. And what you need to understand is that it's the same for me. Bryce is a great pleasure and I'm going to indulge myself and spend Sunday afternoon with him, but you know, Marina, that has to be all.

Love,

Astrid

By early Sunday afternoon, it was cold, but the sun shone brightly, and the entire population of Paris had rushed to the parks. Bryce watched the children throwing snowballs while their parents chatted. Dozens of runners were out in stylish ensembles, although it seemed to Bryce that the French ran in a far more balletic manner than the Americans that he was used to seeing. Young couples were in one another's arms, old couples strolled arm in arm, all taking advantage of the bright, beautiful day. Someone touched his shoulder; he turned and she was there.

Astrid wore a black woolen coat, belted at the waist. Her silky black hair floated out from a red woolen cloche. She wore red leather gloves. Bryce thought about his running shoes, Levi's, and Eddie Bauer parka. She was French; he was American.

"Ready?" she asked.

"You lead, I follow."

They walked along the park and then turned onto a small, quiet street, rue de Fleurus. Astrid stopped and pointed her red leather finger at number 27.

"Here's where we begin," said Astrid. "For thirty-five years the center of modern art and literature in Paris." She looked around the empty street and smiled slyly. "Obviously, I'm telling you a great secret," she whispered. "Nobody knows it or this place would be swarming with tourists, right?"

"Anybody who cared about such things could find out easily. Nobody cares, damn them. Didn't they learn anything in school? Okay, I'll stop ranting - Gertrude Stein lived here?"

"Gertrude and her brother, Leo, refugees from Oakland, California. Alice Toklas was from San Francisco."

"It's remarkable. I had no idea. I thought Stein was from California, but Oakland?"

"She was the one who said, 'There is no there there,' remember? And she was talking about Oakland."

They stared at the number sign and at the plaque beneath it. They turned back and headed for St-Germain-des-Prés. Astrid talked about Picasso and Matisse, Fitzgerald and Hemingway, de Beauvoir and Sartre. Bryce had known that Albert Camus and James Joyce had frequented cafes in the area, but it surprised him to learn that Berthold Brecht had also been there, as well as Truman Capote and Lawrence Durrell.

"That's quite an alumni association," he said, staring at Les Deux Magots. "I wonder what it was really like. When you're young you think it must have been thrilling to wrestle with ideas in public places. I'm feeling older. I suspect that it might have been a bunch of people who thought very highly of themselves and loved to engage in competitive oration."

A guarded smile flickered across her face. "That's a very sad thought. You should be embarrassed to think so cynically."

"Uh-huh. Not that I think my university friends were on the same level, but there's something about people who hold forth that sends me running."

"I don't know. I think we can allow some holding forth from these people. It's not everyone who can say he spent time in a German stalag and then later turned down a Nobel Prize."

"Wow. Who was that?"

"Sartre."

Bryce shook his head. "I shouldn't say anything. I don't know enough about it. But there's nothing that says that somebody who has suffered and turned down prizes can't be an obnoxious person."

Astrid lifted her eyebrows and shrugged. "I haven't personally met anybody who fits your description, but I agree – it's certainly possible. Besides," she added, "I am a bourgeoise who escapes from time to time with literature. He would think very poorly of me."

They walked on. The sun broke through the clouds and the snow on the ground grew whiter.

"I think the Musée Cluny is around here someplace," Bryce said. "I loved the tapestries. Charming. Mysterious. Both charming and mysterious."

"It's true. They are magic. I haven't read any explanation of *à mon seul désir* that satisfies me. Do you have a theory?"

"Oh, God, no. I have no idea what my own sole desire is, much less some allegorical lady from five hundred years ago."

"If you had to name your sole desire, what would it be?"

They walked on while he thought it over. "I don't have a sole desire. Just speaking for myself, love, I guess. But health is a big one. But if I could have a sole desire, why should it be about me? World peace? Some grand concept of justice that is imposed on the whole world? I can't begin to guess. Good thing nobody is offering - the question's too big. Maybe it's a good thing we don't know what the lady's sole desire is. It can remain a universal mystery."

You've been to Notre-Dame?" she asked.

"Of course."

"Then let me take you to the second biggest church in Paris. It's a few hundred years later – only started in the seventeenth century, but it's mysterious, too, but more of an Enlightenment mystery."

They walked until they came to a large open square and an imposing fountain. At one side of the square rose an even more imposing façade of a twin-towered church.

Astrid took his arm. "Saint-Sulpice," she said. "Just wait."

Inside, the church was immense.

"The Marquis de Sade was baptized here," she said softly. "Victor Hugo was married here, and Madame de Montespan was buried here. Not in that order." She stood behind him, held onto his arms and turned him around. He gaped at the organ.

"Six thousand six hundred pipes," she said.

"Not possible."

"But yes. This has been the throne of the great organists of Paris since the seventeenth century."

They walked quietly around, beginning with the Delacroix murals in a side chapel. Eventually, they came to a white obelisk bisected by a line of brass, the famous gnomon. She showed him how the brass line ran down the obelisk to the floor and then across the church. At the spring and autumn equinoxes, the sun's light would pass through a lens set into a south-facing window and strike a copper plate set in the floor. "When you know when the spring equinox is," she explained, "then you can figure out what date Easter falls on."

"It sounds a little woo-woo to me," Bryce said.

"Woo-woo?"

"Superstitious."

"Oh, no. It's a marvel of rationality. Well, maybe a little 'woo-woo' if you insist. It really is magnificent, and I've always found Saint-Sulpice a place of both clarity and mystery. I hate it that it's been slandered by that ridiculous popular novel. They even had to put a sign up here to warn all the tourists that nothing that the book said about the gnomon was true."

Bryce read the inscription at the base of the obelisk: It is thus, Lord, that you give limits to our days, and our entire life is as nothing in your eyes.

"That's grim enough," he said.

"But it's good medicine. Don't you find self-absorption everywhere you look? Aren't there people who you'd like to force to read this every day? Politicians? Rich executives? All those people who think God has favored them because they have power and money? Even present company occasionally not excepted? Just a little bit, every once in a while?"

"Almost everywhere. And me, too, from time to time, I get that. I can't speak for you, just myself. But the self-absorbed, whether they are politicians or billionaires or just my Cousin Brenda, deny the importance of the lives of others, especially of the ones least able to help themselves. I want God not to be like that. I don't need to be more important to God than anybody else, I just don't want some people to count and others not to count."

They left the church, walked through the square, and turned south. Astrid looked at Bryce.

"So, you are a Christian?"

Bryce thought.

"I think you'd have to ask somebody else, preferably God. No, probably not. I mean, 'God' is just a word, a kind of shorthand for some metaphorical idea of creation and some abstract union of justice and love. And then you listen to people talk about Christianity and good luck trying to figure out what it means. And I can't stand the people who just grab all they can, the hell with everybody else. "

"Your politicians call the poor the takers. I assume you don't mean them when you talk about the grabbers."

"You assume right."

"We're too serious," she said. "Time for coffee and pastry, yes?"

"Yes."

But in a patisserie, over coffee and small cakes, Bryce couldn't resist becoming serious again.

"How about you? Are you religious?"

"I like what you said. You have to ask God, I have no idea. That is, I think yes, I probably am, but I also think that nobody else would think so, especially the people who pride themselves on being Christian."

"'Spiritual, but not religious?'"

"Not that, either. I suspect that the people who say that don't much question themselves. Or they just like the emotion, the sentiment. Or they aren't very articulate. Or some combination."

"So, you are . . .?"

"One of those inarticulate people, I guess. I run out of words."

Then they both ran out of words. They stirred their coffee and poked at their cakes. They nibbled, sipped, and avoided looking at one another. Outside it was already dark. She walked back with him until they got to his corner. Against the streetlight, her hair waved out from her hat and shimmered around her face.

"Here I go back to my mother."

"Astrid, I have to ask you a question."

She looked a little alarmed.

"Astrid, are you single?"

She looked to the side, then to the sidewalk. Then she looked straight at him, and he imagined her as an opponent, faced off against him.

"I am single. And very likely to remain so."

"I want to see you again."

"Bryce. I loved this afternoon. I loved being with you. This is the best afternoon I've spent in . . . in as long as I can remember. That doesn't change the fact that I'd rather not see you again."

"Damn! You are like Marina! What? All life is change?"

She suddenly became the Jacqueline of the paintings, fierce and sad. "I'm not like Marina!" Her voice dropped and grew hoarse. "I am – who I must be. Good-bye."

One week was gone. What was he going to do in the next two weeks? He spent the next days retracing their walk, remembering what they talked about at the park, on the rue des Fleurus, on the rue d'Assas, how she looked standing in the winter sunshine in front of the Café de Flore, how it felt to be with her, overwhelmed in Saint-Sulpice and feeling suspended in the infinite lines that measure the cosmos. He thought about the Paris of Alice Toklas and Zelda Fitzgerald and Truman Capote. He wondered what God it might be to whom all His/Her creations were nothing, and wanted to ask her who or what that remote deity might be or mean. He went back to the patisserie for more coffee and cake and sat at the same table that they had sat in before.

In his last days he gave up sight-seeing and just walked. He looked at the façades of buildings without knowing when they were built or why. Or, he went into a Métro station and took a train for a few stops, got off, and walked around. He found open markets that seemed almost accidental. You'd expect to come back in a few hours and find that they had vanished. He bought sweet oranges from North Africa and chatted with the man at the stall. He found himself in charmless neighborhoods, lined with bland concrete buildings, a part of Paris that no tourist raved about. He wondered what it would be like if he moved here, living in the tiny apartment, the neighborhood becoming his new hometown, to become, himself, one of the neighbors, perhaps not as friendly as M. André, but then again, not as cranky as Mme. Mercier. He wondered how it would feel not to live in his own country, to be always a foreigner in jeans and running shoes and parka.

He saved the most obvious tourist attraction for last. On Friday evening he sent her an e-mail. "I leave on Sunday. Meet me tomorrow at the Eiffel Tower at one o'clock for lunch?"

The next day he waited under the great construction until after three o'clock and gave up. The day after that he flew back to the States. By the time he was over the Atlantic the book about the causes of World War I had become too hard for him to read. It was in a foreign language. His three weeks were up.

E-mail from Astrid to Marina:

Don't do me any more favors, all right?
Love,
Astrid

E-mail from Marina to Astrid:

I'm very encouraged to hear that.
Hugs,
Marina

CHAPTER FOUR

Back to real life, he told himself. One dinner and one after-noon with a woman I'll never see again. There seemed to be a voice in his head that belonged to somebody else, somebody from a comic book, somebody from a Roy Lichtenstein ro-mance comic-book painting, a voice that said *Sometimes that's all it takes! A few hours and you just know! You know forever!* He felt as if he had fallen down a well, a mine shaft, a rabbit hole, and he felt foolish to be feeling that way. He thought about The Bookstore of Other Languages. A lifetime of native-speaker fluency for $100,000. And where would that come from? And what would it get him?

He went back to his life. He worked, he bicycled for an hour a day, and from time to time he tackled one of the stack of books he brought back from Paris. It was slow going, look-ing up word after word, but Bryce tried to convince himself that somewhere in his head was the brain of his high school self and somewhere in that brain were four years of French classes. He kept at it.

The Friday Study Group at the Crab Pot took his situation under advisement. The situation, that is, as they heard it from Bryce's carefully edited account of his three weeks in Paris. He told them about the shops, the bookstores, the Cluny tapestries, even about Saint-Sulpice, and then, reluctantly, about Astrid. He couldn't bring himself to tell them any more about The Bookstore of Other Languages. It was too crazy. He had an uncomfortable vision of their exchanging glances, exchanging e-mails privately, and maybe, eventually, doing some sort of horrible, embarrassing intervention.

"I know nothing about women," said Hal, who had been married to Kristie, the owner of the local bookstore, for twelve years and had three children.

"Ugh. Relationships," said Ginnie, recently single yet again. "But you know what? You don't have a relationship. You have a vivid imagination. You know nothing about her and she doesn't want you to know anything, right? I say, give the real world a try."

Ashley, who had a long-term understanding with Carlos, of Lo Tengo, pouted and frowned. "I think this is all Marina's fault," she said.

He felt rootless, unattached. He knew that The Bookstore of Other Languages was there, that he could take another trip. Maybe to Reykjavik or Mexico City or Jaipur. Why not? Why not, he decided, was because his feeling of drifting wasn't about travel. Even if he bought two weeks of language at native speaker level, he would have no sense of attachment, no family ties, no personal history, no political history, no understanding of the country or the culture. Things people took for granted, like, for example, how to talk to people or how to eat would be completely foreign to him. He could go to Arizona and speak Navajo like a native, but so what? He would be a complete stranger there and anywhere else he went. He'd be a freak. At the same time, he began to feel like a stranger here, unattached to his business, his friends, and his town. Bryce settled into a sour mood and remained there.

In March, Linda, announced as always by Merle Haggard, called with plans for his father's seventieth birthday celebration.

"I'm thinking maybe I'll bring in some entertainment," she said.

"Mom, just tell me you're not hiring strippers," he teased.

"Don't be silly! But now that you mention it . . ."

"Mom!"

"Okay, okay. What do you think? A magician? The grandchildren will be there."

"What children? Who else is coming?"

"Sally and Kenny and the boys, Phil and Eric from next door, with Eric's daughter, Tonya, and her daughter, your Uncle Mel, you and me."

"And what about Brenda?"

"Oh, didn't you know? She's back traveling around the Adriatic again."

"No, no, no. This is so wrong. Why on earth would she want to go back there?"

"I'm sure I don't know. Why does Brenda do anything? No, that's not right. She's looking at art."

"Why? Brenda doesn't give a damn about art. The only art she cares about is the art of the handbag. And the wallet, of course."

"Bryce, all I know is that she told Mel that she was looking at ancient art, and Mel told Dad and Dad told me."

"God only knows what she's doing, and He's welcome to keep the information to Himself. Anyway, sure. Get a magician. If you really want to please Dad, get the magician to pull a stripper out of his hat."

"Dad says he's invited a mystery guest and won't tell me who it is. I can't imagine."

Bryce drove to Portland through so much rain that he was alert for signs of flooding on the interstate. He pulled into his parents' driveway as it was beginning to get dark, got his suitcase and wrapped present out of the trunk, and presented himself at the door.

"Bryce! You look so thin!" his mother said as she opened the door. "Your room is all ready for you."

"You're looking beautiful, Mom – you've got a new do. How are you holding up? All ready for the big day tomorrow?"

"Oh, I guess. I canceled my piano students for yesterday and today. I never do that and I hope nobody's mad at me, but they won't be – they just won't practice this week. I'm not doing a big dinner for everybody, just an afternoon party with cake and ice cream and punch, plus champagne for the grown-ups."

Linda paused and looked around the small dining room made smaller by the upright piano at one side. "And I have big plans for party decorations."

"Gonna tell me?"

"Nope. Surprise. Really? You like the curls? I got a new hair stylist."

"It's you and not your hair, but your hair looks great. Brenda hasn't shown up, has she? I really really hope she's not Dad's mystery guest."

"You know your father can't stand Brenda. The nose piercing was bad enough, but the tattoo pushed him over the brink."

"Oh, my God in heaven. What tattoo?"

"Something rude about Albania. Something with the F word, I'm trying not to remember."

"I don't want to imagine."

"But, listen, Bryce. Here's something odd. Stevie called Mel about Brenda being in Albania."

"What? Why?"

"You know Stevie never had anything against our family – just about Brenda. And even though they're divorced, she insisted on keeping his name, and he really doesn't want her making embarrassing headlines and he really doesn't want her embarrassing Nina. I suppose it could interfere with his business – you never know who he's doing business with – but I doubt it. I just think in a way Stevie is just old-fashioned and doesn't want his ex-wife caught doing stupid things."

"She wasn't doing anything embarrassing – all she did was fall into a pothole. And besides, how would he know about her being in Albania?"

"You won't believe it, but she called Stevie and complained about you. She said you got in the way of her business dealings and accused Stevie of sending you to keep an eye on her. Stevie told her she was crazy, but then he called Uncle Mel to ask what was going on. You may hear from him, too."

Bryce shook his head. "This is nuts. I'm going to take my backpack upstairs. Where's Dad?"

"He's planting onion starts in the garden."

Roger was just putting away his tools.

"Bryce! Good to see you. Here, would you take these stakes? I've got the rest."

They walked back to the garden shed, where tools lay on shelves, hung from hooks, or leaned against corners.

"I always thought seventy sounded so old," Roger said. "But I'm pretty much the same as always. Except for the insomnia and the arthritis. But otherwise I feel great. Seventy sounds too old. Glad to be retired, of course."

And that was Roger, Bryce thought. Always seeing three sides to every question.

"I just wanted to confess," Bryce said, "that if it turns out that Mom didn't hire a stripper for your party it's my fault. I told her not to."

"Too bad. It would have been educational for the children. Just as long as it isn't a goddamn clown. Not that clowns mean to be creepy. People who want to be clowns must lack some key awareness of how they're coming over. But, then, there are people who like clowns, so I suppose they must kind of be made for each other, each lacking the same key ability to perceive creepiness."

Bryce enjoyed his father's habit of holding up an idea and examining it from every angle. "Maybe we are the ones lacking," he suggested. "Maybe we lack some gene that allows us to enjoy clowns. It could be, you know, that this gene that we lack is essential to our family's long-time survival."

Roger nodded. "It could be."

Bryce thought that dinner alone with his parents the night before the party might be the best part of the weekend. His mother checked the mirror frequently, questioning her new curly hair; his dad joked more than usual – maybe he really was uneasy about turning seventy – but they were at ease with one another, and dinner was a pleasure. Roger cleaned up after dinner, as usual, and Bryce assisted.

"Be sure to put the food scraps in the compost can," Roger reminded him. "Sometimes I think we should get chickens – we could feed them the food scraps and get them back again in the form of eggs."

"You already get them back in the form of vegetables and flowers," Bryce reminded him.

"True enough."

"Dad. We're alone. You can tell me. Who's the mystery guest."

"You'll be mad at me."

"Oh my God, who?"

"Sheila."

"Sheila! Why?"

"Well, I know that she left you, but it's been a few years, and I thought maybe you'd want to catch up. I ran into her again at the grocery store last week and it seemed like a good idea. She was always friendly to us."

"Why would I want to catch up? Ask how her weaving is coming along? Ask how Woofie is doing? What?"

"So, you don't think it was a good idea?"

Bryce took a deep breath. Maybe it wasn't so crazy. Maybe he could ask her about her weaving or about Woofie.

"No, it's okay, Dad. I mean, it's not something I would have asked you to do, but it's okay."

"Well! That's a relief. I didn't ask if she's still single."

The next morning Bryce vacuumed for Linda, then took Roger out for a long lunch so that Linda could get ready for the party without male interference. When they got back, they found that she had hung glittery cardboard lightning bolt shapes from the dining room ceiling and suspended a life-sized cardboard flying Superman over the table. Over the face she had glued a photograph of Roger. By two o'clock, Linda was looking nervously at her watch and watching the window for the first cars.

Guests started to come in the room, gasping at the decorations and laughing, to Linda's extreme gratification. Phil and Eric arrived first, with Eric's daughter, Tonya, and her little girl, Isabelle. Sally and Kenny arrived from across town, with Cole and Connor. Uncle Mel came, and last, looking a little embarrassed, Sheila. Linda brought in a blue cake with a shield-shaped logo with a big red R instead of an S, and Roger blew out the two candles, a 7 and a 0. The cake was cut, Bryce scooped ice cream, Uncle Mel opened a bottle of champagne, the kids got punch, and then the business of opening presents began. Roger opened them all with grace and humor, but still, Bryce believed his father was truly pleased with his gift, a book of essays on gardening.

Before Bryce had a chance to say hello to Sheila – their eyes had met when she walked into the room – Mr. Marker, the caricaturist, arrived and set up an easel, a large pad of paper, and an array of colored markers. "Who'll be first to have their portrait drawn?" he asked. People looked at the floor. With an experienced eye, Mr. Marker identified young Connor as his first volunteer. "Make believe you can go anywhere in the world!" he said to Connor, "where would it be?"

"Disneyland," squealed Connor, and soon, amid dramatic flourishes, there was a reasonable approximation of Connor shaking hands with Mickey Mouse in front of the magic castle. This initial success brought more volunteers, and soon there was a picture of Linda at the White House, Uncle Mel with cash stuffed in his pockets at Las Vegas, and Tonya in a grass skirt in Hawaii.

"Who hasn't done it yet?" Mr. Marker asked. Someone said, "You go, Sheila," and Sheila said, "Oh, nobody's gone to Paris yet! I'll go there," and Bryce watched as Sheila appeared in high heels, trench coat, and beret in front of the Eiffel Tower.

"And where do you want to go, sir?" Mr. Marker asked Bryce. With a suddenly buzzing head and aching heart, Bryce announced fraudulently that he couldn't wait to go to Italy, and was rewarded with a picture of himself eating spaghetti in front of the leaning tower of Pisa.

In the chaos of the departures, Sheila approached Bryce.

"Look, I'm sorry I came. Your dad invited me and I didn't want to say no."

"Oh, I get it. I understand, and yeah, I'm feeling a little awkward, but it really is good to see you. I'm driving back tomorrow. Do you want to have breakfast with me at Doreen's? It would be good. I'd like to hear how things are going with you."

"Okay. Yeah. It can't be too late. I have a job. Say eight?"

"Great. Thanks. See you then."

In the evenings, Doreen's Diner was the scene of high school dates, the place the gang went after skating or games or the movies, and that was how Bryce remembered it. In the morning it was the place where old guys met to drink coffee and talk politics. Walking into Doreen's, Bryce felt as if he could see his youth and his old age all at once.

Doreen had died since Bryce had left Portland, but nobody had had the heart to change the name, even though the diner was now owned by Candy, who had been working there since her own high school days, before Bryce was born.

Sheila had cut her hair. Instead of a long mass of curls, she now had a cloud of brown ringlets that quivered gently around her face. Bryce thought about the last time he saw Astrid, in front of the streetlight, her hair waving out from her hat and making an aura around her face. Sheila had started to go gray. Bryce fingered his mustache, where he was also finding gray hairs. They slid into a booth, and a waitress that Bryce didn't recognize came over with menus.

"Hi, Sheila, how's it going?"

"Fine, Bets. This is Bryce Hanford. Do you remember him from high school?"

"Oh, my God! Bryce! I remember you from algebra class. You were one of the stars! Oh, Mr. Elling! So scary!"

Bryce felt as if he were required to be slightly ashamed of himself.

"Good to see you, Bets."

"So! Sheila, you want the regular? What'll it be for you, Bryce?"

"Do you still do huevos rancheros?"

"Sure thing."

"Coffee for you both?"

"Sure."

Bryce broke the silence.

"What's your job?"

Sheila shrugged and her curls bounced around her face. "I'm working in a craft gallery and showing my weaving there, too. It's kind of a co-op, but I've also got a job there keeping track of inventory and sales. I'm sort of the bookkeeper, the registrar, the assistant to the director. It's cool. I'm making a living, well, a small living, but a living. I have a salary and health insurance, and then I sell something every once in a while. It feels very good."

More silence. Sheila broke it.

"How are you, Bryce? Still with your nose stuck in a book?"

"Oh, you know, always that. I put in raised beds and plant-ed vegetables, but the deer ate them."

"I could have told you that," she said quickly, and then stopped. "Sorry. What else?"

Bryce took a breath. "I've been traveling. I went to Albania to rescue my loathsome cousin Brenda."

"I remember Brenda. She always was loathsome."

"So then I did some more traveling." He told her about Marina, about going to Paris, a little about Astrid, and nothing at all about The Bookstore of Other Languages.

"Mr. Marker should have put you in Paris. I don't know why I said I wanted to go there, I just wasn't thinking. I'd rather go to New Zealand or Iceland, someplace where they have great wool."

Bets came with huevos rancheros for Bryce, a blueberry muffin for Sheila, and more coffee for each.

"Hey, Bets," Sheila said, "Bryce is a world traveler. He went to Paris."

"Wow. How was it?"

"I can tell you that no matter how many pictures you see of the Eiffel Tower, it's way bigger than you think it's going to be. It's gigantic."

"That must have been cool!"

"It was."

Bets looked around the room for empty coffee cups and went off to refill them.

They ate in silence, and finally Bryce spoke.

"Okay, truth or dare. Seeing anybody?"

More silence.

"Yeah. Yes, I am. He's nice. His name is Bruce, actually, which is kind of weird, you know, Bruce - Bryce. He runs a printing company and does letterpress art that he shows in the gallery. He plays bluegrass banjo."

"Oh. Good. Very good." Bryce almost added that he had tried and failed to enjoy bluegrass, but caught himself in time.

More silence.

"How's Woofie?"

"Woofie's fine."

Sheila finished her muffin and grabbed her parka. "I have to run. Got to open the gallery." She leaned over and kissed him on the cheek. "Bye."

On the long drive home Bryce thought about women. He was shocked by how attractive he found Sheila. He found those new short curls irresistible, how they framed her heart-shaped face and how they trembled with any motion she made. He thought about trembling, about how they had both trembled the first time they had come together, how they had trembled so hard they couldn't undress. The echo of that long ago shuddering of passion seemed to persist all these years later in the tiny vibrations of the curls around her face. He remembered his younger self, drowning in their coming together. He knew, though, that the bluegrass-playing artist was the person she should be with. It was perfect. He, Bryce, was never someone Sheila would need. The guilty thought came to him that just possibly, she wasn't what he needed.

It wasn't that he couldn't go on after Sheila left. There was Marina. He had deliciously drowned in Marina, too, and then a few months later, she was gone with a wave and a smile. She was beautiful, there was nothing malicious in her, but what had he been thinking? Well . . . thinking. It was uncomfortable to ask himself if he had deliberately refused to see Marina for who she was because he was, damn it, desperate. Why couldn't he be more like Marina? Affectionate, sensual, happy, what was wrong with that?

If he could be just a little more like Marina and a little less like, well, himself, life would be easier. For starters, he could turn to his old friend Ginnie. Why not? She would enjoy it, would appreciate an affectionate, sensual, happy vacation from her recent break-up. He knew, though, that he would always want to be friends with Ginnie, and would never want to be anything else. Damn. Damn again.

And then there was Astrid. Now he was completely lost. One evening, one afternoon. Just that. And now the memory of those hours forced him to face the fact that any idea he ever had of being that light-hearted, easy-going person whose life seemed so desirable was obviously make-believe. It was bad enough not see Marina for who she was, but he couldn't even see who he was. It was Astrid who forced him to this self-examination. What would it be like to spend days, months, years with someone whose very way of being in the world allowed him to be aware of his own way of being in the world?

A few days after he had returned from Portland, Bryce did indeed get a call from his former cousin-in-law. An international businessman, Stevie was never in a hurry, always polite, and, seemingly, always got what he wanted. After inquiring about Bryce's health, his business, and then about Roger and Linda's health, Stevie became serious.

"Bryce, I'm calling because I'm concerned about Brenda and what she was doing in the Adriatic."

"Stevie – I have no idea what she was doing, except for falling in a pothole in the sidewalk and winding up in the hospital. Plus wasting days of my time and thousands of Mel's dollars. Besides, Stevie, this is awkward for me, but I wouldn't feel great about filling you in on Brenda's doings, no matter how misguided."

"Bryce, listen to me. I don't need you do anything you're not comfortable with. I have people. I could send someone to spy on Brenda. Easiest thing in the world. But I don't need a spy. I need you to help me prevent her from doing something worse than misguided. From doing something illegal and dangerous, not to mention embarrassing to her family. Also embarrassing to me. I do not want to see a Bongiorno on trial. And I definitely don't want Nina to see her mother on trial."

"Okay, now you're scaring me. Stevie, what is going on?"

"I wish I knew. Here's what I do know: after Brenda called me to complain about your upsetting her plans in Albania, I started asking around. I have . . . well, let's call them family connections as well as business concerns in Italy. Those people have connections in Greece. Finally I heard, but not from reliable sources, that Brenda was in Greece and Albania talking with dealers in antiquities."

"Stevie, maybe she was shopping. I mean, you know, she does love expensive things."

"Nobody knows that better than I do. But, Bryce – listen to me. The people that she was rumored to have spoken with don't deal with housewives out to buy antique jewelry or redecorate their condo in Santa Fe. They deal with people who want to buy artifacts looted from archaeological digs. Or, let's say, 'lost' from private collections. Or even museum collections."

"Oh. Oh, God."

"Exactly."

Stevie allowed a few moments of silence.

"Bryce. All I'm asking is for you to stay in touch. I'll be talking with some other people, but if Brenda should call on you again, here's a number where you can text me and I'll call you back."

Bryce reached for pen and paper.

One brilliantly sunny day in May, Marina showed up. It was getting a bit dreary in Oz, and she missed island life. Bryce looked at her long silky black hair and blue eyes and saw her aunt.

"I missed the island and I missed you, too," she said to Bryce. The sound of Marina's voice took him back six months. It was the sound of Astrid's voice.

"Let's go get coffee," he said. "I want to talk with you."

"Oooh, you sound so scary," she said with a grin.

He made a face at her.

She lifted her dark, arched eyebrows and laughed and he was in Paris on a Sunday afternoon.

They went to Mr. D's and ordered coffee. Marina had a biscotti. Bryce was still staring at her hair.

"What?" she said. "What is it?"

"It's so amazing. You look like your aunt, you sound like her, but you're so different."

"She told me you met her!"

"A little. She showed me around one afternoon."

"She loves to drag people around Paris and show them where things happened. I bet you got the disasters of the Commune, yes?"

"No, I got the Lost Generation. Then Saint-Sulpice."

"Oh, she's nuts about Saint-Sulpice."

"I think I might be a bit nuts about Saint-Sulpice myself."

"Oh, Jesus. The thing with Astrid is she's so damn serious about everything. I bet she went on and on about that wicked novel. It was entertainment for God's sake. She should just let up. Weren't you exhausted afterwards?"

"No, no I wasn't. It was electrifying. I mean, it was as if I were connected somehow to the world in a way that I hadn't realized before."

Marina rolled her eyes. "If you say so. So what happened? Does this mean I'm wasting my time hoping to get back together with you?"

"Will you be broken-hearted if I say yes?"

"Do I strike you as the broken-hearted type?"

"You strike me as a woman who would shrug, face it that things had changed, not be mad at me, and would go out and find somebody with a little more oomph."

"Well . . . there is a guy who works on the ferries. Very fit, oh my goodness. Blond. A Viking."

"That would be Kurt."

"SO yummy."

"You'll be a great couple."

She got up from the table, kissed him on the mouth, smiled, and walked out the door.

E-mail from Marina to Astrid:

Dearest, sweetest Astrid,

You are incredibly stupid! Bryce has eyes only for you. I know. I tried flirting with him and got nowhere. Just flat out nowhere. Which is fine because there is a very tasty fellow who works on the ferry and the way I'm looking at things now, he's my target; he's doomed.

But you! You and Bryce are both so serious you'll never get together unless someone forces you. I'm going to be thinking this over and I'm sure I'm going to have a brilliant idea and will rope you both together.

Love always,

Marina

At the Crab Pot, Bryce brought the question to the Friday Study Group. "Let's get serious," he said. "Are you who you are and you can't change? Is there an essential you that might learn something here and there, but is never going to change in any substantial way?"

"You're asking an English major this question?" asked Ginnie. "Everybody who has studied any of the humanities in the last thirty years knows that the person is a construct, and its essence is an unreliable, multivalent, construction. And no, nobody really changes very much, especially after they're thirty. They are who they are."

"Same here," said Ashley. "You think historians don't study postmodern theory? The answer is that your question does not exist. The discourse you need to theorize about it is no longer relevant. The "you" produces texts, but that's really all you can say. And of course nobody really changes. Much."

"So grateful I studied math," said Hal. "Grateful every day and especially at this very moment. No. People don't change. They are who they are. Except for hairlines." He ran his hand over his scalp.

"And hair color," said Ginnie of the one long, silver tress.

"Okay, we answered your question," said Ashley. "You owe us. What's going on?"

"Marina's back."

Six eyes rolled, three jaws dropped, and a trio of voices said "NO."

"Oh, cut it out. Here's the question. I don't really want to get back together with her. Is it that I've changed or that I'm closer to my essential self?"

"We salute you, we congratulate you, and we say that you are at least one drink short."

"Oh, okay." said Bryce, "My round," and went back to the bar.

CHAPTER FIVE

Marina did take up with Kurt, and they were a noticeable pair: she tall and slender, with long straight black hair and blue eyes, he with sun-bleached blonde hair, lantern jaw, and a compass rose tattoo on his sizable upper arm. Marina had picked up her former massage practice at the clinic, with recommendations from Dr. Valerie, and with earlier clients happy to return to her skilled kneadings and manipulations. She also returned to her former apartment, a loft over a chandlery at the Eliza Island Marina. She dropped back into Island life as effortlessly as she had entered it the year before and left it six months later.

Bryce saw Marina and Kurt sometimes at the Crab Pot, and from time to time met Marina for coffee or a beer, both for her company and because he hoped to hear something about Astrid. He had begun to think of Marina as a wayward relative whom he needed to spend a little time with just to make sure she was okay. That she was one of the most self-sufficient people he had ever known made no difference. He felt like a family elder and had begun to act like one.

Meanwhile his own life went on. After threatening several times to abandon the school district and its endless, uninformed ambitions for a new IT system, Bryce had convinced them to aim for a reasonable goal and to understand that even that would cost more than they wanted it to. He had also had to guide their vision for software and to encourage them to accept that to choose any one system was to limit the range of software that they could employ. Their last unreasonable ambition was to entice him to sell his business and become a school district employee, but eventually they had given up.

As a result of the added work with the school district, Bryce and Justin had become overwhelmed, so Bryce took on Kendra Heglund to keep up with the rest of the business. Kendra had a recent degree in computer science but no ambition to elbow her way up the ladder of a big corporation. With her long braids, long skirts, and freckles, she looked like what she was, a friendly, small-town young woman, pleased to get a job in a small-town business.

Marina began to treat him, Bryce felt, as he treated the school district, as if he needed expert advice. Over coffee, she advised him it was time to move on from the stationary bike.

"Good for you," she said, "you've made a start, but you need to try something else, at least add something to the mix."

Bryce frowned. "Like what?"

"Pick a card, any card: martial arts, like kickboxing or aikido, lots of options. How about weight training? Yoga? How about just getting off the bike and running?"

"Too bad we don't have a gym on the Island."

"To tell the truth, Kurt's thinking of opening a gym. It's time."

"Aha! You are rounding up customers for him!"

"I guess, but really, I'm talking about you. You need to branch out. You're doing aerobics, but not much in the way of balance or flexibility, or really even strength training, except your legs."

"I could try yoga, I guess. Ginnie tells me I should, but where? Marina, I just can't get myself to go to a yoga studio called the Blue Heaven Consciousness Center. I just couldn't make my feet go over the threshold of a place with a name like that."

"What I'm going to suggest is totally ungodly. It's probably illegal. But how about I get you a DVD? You could try it out."

"Okay. Just as long as nobody can watch me."

So he added the DVD, which was mostly helpful in making it clear to him that he could improve his flexibility and balance. At coffee at Mr. D's, he complained to Marina, and she shrugged.

"You know what balance poses teach, don't you?" she asked.

"They teach you to be better balanced?"

"Yeah, eventually. Mostly they teach humility."

"Finally something makes sense. I think I'd like to try a class. Just not at Blue Heaven."

Marina smiled. "Kurt's friend Casey is starting to lead a yoga practice on Mondays and Wednesdays before work and on Tuesdays and Thursdays after work. I can get you a flyer. It's vinyasa."

"Vin-what-a?"

"Yoga comes in different flavors. This is just a flavor."

Bryce didn't give up the bike, but added Casey's yoga twice a week. Marina said she was proud of him. Ginnie was miffed that he wasn't going to Blue Heaven Consciousness Center, but she got over it.

Bryce added more unstructured activity. He went on a couple of hikes with Hal and his boys. He went fishing a couple of times with Carlos. Kurt started cautiously with his idea of opening a gym, beginning with a weekend karate dojo, but just as Bryce was unable to join the Blue Heaven Consciousness Center, so he was equally unable to go to a karate studio with the motto "I'm Gonna Belt Ya!" Curious about Marina's comment, he started reading about the Franco-Prussian War and the ensuing horrors of the Commune.

Bryce met Marina at the Crab Pot one evening and found her uncharacteristically quiet. They got their beers at the bar and she led him to a quiet table. They sipped in silence which Bryce finally broke.

"Open up, Marina. Tell your Uncle Bryce all about it."

Bryce watched astonished as a tear slid down Marina's cheek.

"Marina! Tell me! What?"

She sniffed and took a gulp of her beer.

"I have breast cancer."

He fell into icy water.

"I'm here. Tell me."

"Valerie was always giving me a hard time that I was working out of her clinic and I ought to be getting check-ups like we keep telling people to do. But I didn't. I mean, I'm totally and completely healthy, my blood pressure is text-book perfect, my cholesterol is perfect. I knew I was healthy."

"When was the last time you checked?"

"Four years ago and I'm telling you, everything is perfect!" She sighed. "Except it isn't."

"What happened?"

"I had a fucking mammogram and I have a fucking tumor and now I have to have fucking surgery. I'm seeing a fucking surgeon in Seattle on Monday and Kurt can't come with me, he has to work."

"I'll come with you," said Bryce, and Marina put her head down on the table and sobbed. Bryce lay his hand tenderly on her head and thought harshly about Kurt. "Of course I will," he said.

E-mail from Marina to Astrid:

Dearest Astrid,

I don't even know how to begin. I need you very much, but this has nothing to do with Bryce, except it probably will, but that is nothing I planned. Oh, I sound so confused!

Oh, Astrid, dear, you will be upset to hear that I have breast cancer. Bryce is taking me into Seattle tomorrow to consult with a surgeon. In the worst of all worlds, I will have some horrible form of advanced breast cancer and will die; in the best of all possible worlds, it will be a little nothing and I'll bounce out of my hospital bed and go dancing. In the most likely world, though, I'll lose a

*breast, maybe two, have chemo and radiation and God knows
what else.*

*Astrid, if I do have to do all that, will you please come? A few
weeks while I recover from surgery and get started with chemo – if
I have to – would be so wonderful. You will know more what to do
than anyone else. I trust you more than anybody.*

Is there any chance?

Yes or no, I send you much love and know I can rely on yours.

Marina

The next day was a Friday. The night before, Bryce had asked
Justin and Kendra to meet him in the shop for breakfast before
work. He would see the Study Group that evening.

Kendra had settled in nicely at work, and turned out to be
particularly good at talking with walk-in customers. Her warm
smile, freckles, and braids somehow reassured people to the
point where she could charm them into concentrating on describing their problems in detail. With Kendra at the desk,
Bryce had been spend more time calling on local businesses,
including the school district, and Justin was free to do what he
did best, work on problem computers. He worked like a detec-
tive, eliminating false leads, identifying meaningful clues, and
tracking down the faulty element and fixing it. He did it in the
shop and on house calls and did it quickly and accurately. The
business was in great shape.

Bryce had never called a meeting like this, and Justin and
Kendra eyed him warily as he walked in the door. He had
brought their coffees, just as they liked them, and an array of

pastries. They looked at one another, then looked back at Bryce.

"Oh, stop," Bryce scolded them. "You're fine, I'm fine, the business is fine," and he handed out the coffees and paper napkins.

"Here's the deal. We're all fine, we're better than fine. You're great, you're fine. But my friend Marina is not fine. This is a small town, word gets around very fast, and Marina agrees with me that there's not much point in keeping secrets, and besides, you've both met Marina. She doesn't have secrets. She doesn't really care what people know about her."

Justin and Kendra nodded.

"Marina has breast cancer," said Bryce, and Justin and Kendra gasped.

"Yeah. Extremely crappy. Right now Marina needs friends, and through some strange process, I've wound up as her best friend here. So – I'm going to need time off. Instead of going to the boss asking for extra time, I'm coming to you guys. What if I take a day a week off? What if I take off early in the afternoon? What do we have to do to make this work out and keep the business healthy?"

By the time the lattes were drunk and the fritters eaten, they had a plan.

"And also," Bryce said, "I want you to know that I've called my insurance agent, and I'm reviewing your health insurance. Mine, too. This is all suddenly far more real than it was a week ago."

That evening, the Study Group also gasped.

"I don't even have any idea what I might wind up asking you to do," said Bryce, "I just wanted to fill you in on where we were and say I might be asking for something sometime."

"How's Marina?" asked Ashley. "I mean right now."

"Last night was the only time I have ever known her to cry," answered Bryce, "and my money says it will be the last. She doesn't have bravado – she has genuine courage, I think. She really is brave. She's going to face whatever she needs to face."

"When will you have a plan?"

"First surgery, then the plan, I think, but I'll know more tomorrow. Valerie recommended an oncologist and a surgeon over at St. Olaf Hospital. We're seeing the surgeon tomorrow. We'll be going back and forth to the mainland for a while."

"How's the business? You need any help there?"

"Justin and Kendra are all over it."

"You know," said Ginnie, "they're young. Marina is young. They probably don't have friends who have gone through this. I have one friend who is ten years out and doing fine. I have – had – another friend who didn't do so well."

"I guess I've been lucky," said Bryce. "This is the closest I've ever come to a life-threatening illness."

"Here's the only thing I know," said Hal. "Don't try to cheer them up. I had a friend who had prostate cancer and when some guy told him that everything happens for a reason, he pasted him. Bad timing because my friend had an IV in his arm at the time, but still."

"I have every confidence in Marina's ability to stick up for herself. I hate to think what would happen to anybody who tried to tell her that that which does not kill us makes us stronger."

"Bryce, seriously. Keep in touch. Let us know what's going on," said Ashley. "That's an order."

"Yes, Ma'am."

On Monday morning, Bryce and Marina drove onto one ferry, then another, and finally to Anacortes, on the mainland, where they drove to hospital, negotiated a confusing parking structure, and finally emerged from the car. Marina checked in at a large reception area, and they took an elevator to the fifteenth floor. From the windows they could see west across the city to the harbor, to Bainbridge Island, and then to the far away Olympic Mountains. Bryce remembered his own recent experience in this same hospital, his terror a year-and-a-half ago when he saw Dr. Branch, the terror that had quickly dissolved into comical shaky relief. This was not going to happen for Marina.

Marina's name was called and they were shown into an exam room. After a few minutes, the door opened, and a woman who had to be the smallest surgeon in the entire world walked in.

"Hello," she said. "Ms. Ollivier? I'm Dr. Yee."

Dr. Yee reviewed what they knew so far. She explained that during the surgery, they would remove the tumor and check to see whether the cancer cells had moved to the lymph system. The oncologist would recommend treatment depending on what they discovered in surgery. When Dr. Yee brought up the subject of a mastectomy, Marina interrupted.

"I've already decided. I wouldn't fiddle around and do things half-way. Bryce will tell you. If there's any doubt – take it!"

Bryce nodded, and recognized that he wouldn't have expected any other answer from Marina.

Dr. Yee explained much more, about staging, about possible breast reconstruction; she encouraged Marina to ask questions and answered each question with gentle directness.

"I'll see you on Thursday, then," said Dr. Yee, and left the room.

From there they went to an appointment with the anesthesiologist, who asked all sorts of questions about Marina's health, especially about allergies, and explained the usual anesthesia that he used with this surgery.

Leaving his office, they were both feeling overwhelmed.

Marina said, "Bryce. Here's the thing. I won't know anything more until after surgery, after pathology, after I talk with the oncologist. Right now, all I know is that I could die. I can't think any more today."

They went out for a late expensive lunch at a restaurant overlooking Elliott Bay. The sun glittered on the water, sailboats glided across the bay. They didn't speak much, but allowed the view, the good food, the wine, and their silent companionship to take the sharpest edges off of the day's anxieties. It was only on the last ferry home that Bryce asked the question that had hovered unasked over the day.

"What's going on with Kurt?"

"We broke up. He said that my breast cancer was too much of a negative for him to assimilate and that it was a tough choice, but his primary responsibility was to take care of himself. I told him if there was any justice in the world he'd die because his heart shriveled up into dust and I kicked him out."

"I'm here."

"I know you are. I'm counting on you, but you can't do everything. I don't know what I'm looking at, but it could be months of chemo and radiation and God knows what. I have to make a plan. I'm working on it. It's complicated."

"Want to tell me?"

"Not now."

On Wednesday evening, Bryce and Marina went back to Seattle and checked into a hotel near the hospital. Once in their room, they put their arms around one another and stood weeping. Exhausted, they spent the rest of the night in their clothes, curled up together on the bed, his hand cupped around the breast that was to disappear so soon. Early the next morning they went to the hospital, where Marina filled out forms and then eventually disappeared, and it seemed to Bryce as if she had been swallowed by a monster, who would gnaw at her and eventually spit her out, in what condition he could not imagine.

Hours went by. Bryce went to the coffee shop and remembered the mother and daughter he had seen there the year before, the girl in pale pink, with her hair in a perfect pattern of corn rows. He himself had been giddy, floating on a crest of euphoria at the news of his own good health, of his release from panic. Now he was pushing real panic away. He thought about the Greek god Pan, who could induce sudden unreasoning fear that caused herds to stampede or the lonely traveler to cower in terror, and whose name we invoke every time we use the word "panic."

He went back to the waiting room. The woman with a baby and toddler who was waiting there earlier was gone, and so was the shaky, long-bearded man with two canes. Other people had taken seats, leafing through magazines or staring and poking at their cell phones. A teenage boy sat frowning at a table with a jigsaw puzzle. Bryce reached into his backpack and pulled out *The Remains of the Day*, not at all sure he'd be able to escape into any novel.

A woman with a suitcase walked into the room and went to the desk, probably to inquire about a patient. He returned to his book, but a few minutes later the woman was standing in front of him. Smiling at him.

"Astrid!"

She bit her lip and looked to one side. She sat down next to him, looked at the swirling patterns in the carpet, and said nothing. Bryce couldn't speak, either. He breathed and listened to his heart pounding her name in every double beat.

He looked at her. "What happened?"

She started in French. "Marina m'a écrit la semaine dernière . . ." but Bryce stopped her.

"Astrid. My French . . . isn't what it was. Could we speak in English?"

She stared at him. "Your French is wonderful. What's happening?"

"Just tell me in English."

"Well . . ." She paused. "All right. Marina wrote me. She wrote me last week and asked me if it was possible for me to come take care of her. Everything fell into place amazingly quickly. I took a leave of absence from the lycée, and I'm here."

"What about your mother?"

"She went back to Brittany and is staying with her brother and sister-in-law. I found a tenant for the apartment that you stayed in, and I'm here. I never would have thought it would be so easy."

She paused again. "What happened with your French?"

"Astrid, it's a long story and not really believable. Could I not explain right now?"

She reached over and squeezed his hand. "I think we're probably dealing with all we can right now. We don't need to add anything else, right?"

"Right."

They sat and waited together. Bryce needed, every so often, to turn and stare at her, convincing himself that she was truly there. She was there. It was her blue eyes, dark hair, straight nose, broad cheekbones, her arching eyebrows. It was her swooping lilting voice, so like Marina's. He closed his eyes and willed himself to believe that he was so near her.

"Mr. Hanford? Ms. Ollivier?"

Dr. Yee stood in the doorway and they hurried to her.

"Marina is fine, surgery went fine. We did do a mastectomy. We got all of the tumor, but we'll have to wait for pathology to give us a stage. Her oncologist will be able to tell her much more next week."

Astrid looked at Bryce, then at Dr. Yee.

"I don't even know how I feel," she said.

Dr. Yee's face relaxed a bit. "That sounds absolutely normal, from my experience," she said. "Now here's some advice. Marina has had major surgery. She did fine. We'll keep her here overnight and she can go home tomorrow. She'll need to rest a great deal. Many patients – and she may not be one of them – find that waiting for pathology is one of the most difficult steps. Take your cues from her, but know that while her body is healing from the surgery, the stress on her emotions may be quite acute."

"We understand," said Bryce. "We'll do our best."

Dr. Yee smiled. "She's pretty woozy – that's a medical term – right now, but you could visit her."

"Thank you, Doctor Yee."

Marina was indeed woozy. They sat with her for a while, each holding a hand. Nurses came and checked on things, measured other things. Marina opened her eyes, saw Astrid, and smiled. "Tu es venue," she whispered. "You came."

"Oui, chérie, je suis içi."

"Ah, bon," and she closed her eyes.

Her IV stood beside her bed. Bryce noticed a wound and a lump on Marina's chest a couple of inches below her collar bone. He stopped a nurse and asked him about it.

"Oh, that's her port."

"Her port?"

"It lies under the skin and it delivers the chemo directly to the heart. It makes the chemo sessions easier."

"Will it always be there?"

"Oh, no, it comes out after all the chemo treatments are over."

Bryce felt a little sick. He looked across the hospital bed to Astrid.

"What's happening?" he asked. "Does anybody have a plan?"

"I don't know. Marina told me where you were staying and I booked a room there. I'll be going home with Marina tomorrow. Do you have room in your car for me and my suitcase?"

"Sure."

"Well, then."

"Can I take you out to dinner?"

"Thank you. Yes."

They gave a last good-bye kiss to a sleeping Marina, Bryce picked up Astrid's suitcase, they turned to leave, and they stood in the doorway for one more look. Then they went to Bryce's car in the parking garage, pulled out, and drove slowly, scanning the neighborhood for a restaurant. Seeing a sign for "Bella Natalia," they looked at one another and nodded. Inside, they ordered a bottle of prosecco and slumped into their chairs.

"Where to begin?" asked Bryce.

"Tell me about your arrangements for Marina."

"I'd rather you tell me why you wouldn't see me again in Paris."

"Oh." She lifted her eyebrows and smiled. "And then there's why you aren't speaking French. First you speak it, but you don't tell me how you learned it; now you don't speak it and you don't want to talk about that, either."

Bryce winced. "Astrid, I just can't. Not now. I'll tell you, I promise."

She shrugged and pursed her lips. "Hmm. It seems that unlike Marina, we each have secrets."

The waiter came with their wine, they ordered their dinners, and turned back to the safe topic, how to care for Marina, who would leave the hospital tomorrow with pain medication, a handful of printed instructions, and a cloud of doubt and worry. Astrid could help with pain management, range of motion exercises, shopping, cooking, cleaning, and loving her. Bryce could drive them wherever they needed to go, and could fill in wherever possible.

They ran out of conversation at the same time that their dinners arrived. They were both hungry and they turned to their food with relief.

The next morning they returned to the hospital and collected a slightly less woozy Marina, tucked her carefully into the back seat, with pillows supporting her wherever possible, and made the long trip back to Eliza Island.

CHAPTER SIX

The next day was a Saturday. Bryce went to work as usual, where Kendra and Justin greeted him with a little embarrassment, unsure of how much they ought to ask or not ask.

"I have to tell you," he began, "I'm learning about all sorts of things that I never knew existed and that I never ever wanted to learn about. But there it is. Real life lands on you and what are you going to do?"

They were nice young people – they appreciated his generous attitude; they were still young enough to be unable to imagine that they themselves might be called on one day to emulate it, much less need to call on it. A customer walked in the door with a laptop under her arm, followed by a sad teenager with a cracked cell phone screen. The workday began, and between tasks, Bryce asked himself when or if he should call Marina. Later in the morning, Astrid walked into the shop.

"I'm here as a customer," she announced. "I need a phone."

"You came to the right place – it's on the house. Have you met Justin and Kendra? I have to confess, Kendra knows more about these phones than I do. Kendra, would you please outline the possibilities for Astrid and confuse her no more than strictly necessary? But make sure she doesn't sign up for service with you-know-who."

Kendra nodded. "I'll only take her to the very first circle of hell, I promise."

Sometime later Astrid left, working phone in hand. Bryce saw her to the door, and turned to see the questioning faces of his employees.

"Yes?" they chorused.

"She's Marina's aunt."

Justin and Kendra exchanged glances.

"No, really," he said, and explained enough to prevent their asking more questions, although perhaps not quite enough to prevent their speculating on their own time. Justin and Kendra had much to talk over, and after work they continued their discussion over beer and enchiladas at Lo Tengo.

Bryce had missed the Friday Study Group the evening before, and during the day his friends either called or dropped by the shop to ask about Marina. He became practiced in telling just enough of the story. At the end of the day, he called Astrid on her new phone, and asked if he could pick up any groceries for them, but it seems that they were doing fine. Astrid had used Marina's bicycle to go around the town getting whatever they had needed. Bryce had a few words with Marina, who was tired and in some pain, but was alert. By tomorrow she planned to start exercises. As a massage therapist, she had a good working knowledge of anatomy, and was eager to put it to use in her own healing. After a word of gratitude to Bryce, she gave the phone back to Astrid.

"Astrid, I need some direction, here," Bryce said into the phone. "You're here now, I think I can still help, but you and Marina have to draw the lines. I can't. You have to tell me – may I stop by every day and see how you're doing? When we go to Seattle next week to see the oncologist do I go into the exam room with you? Or wait for you? What?"

"I understand. Let me talk with Marina and we'll talk with you. Bryce, you're part of the team. We can't do without you. We'll make a plan."

Bryce sighed. "Everybody is making a plan. I guess it's good. I don't know what to say. I'm in your hands."

"I'll call you tomorrow. I promise."

Early the next morning Astrid called and asked to meet him.

"Sure," he said. "We could meet for coffee, or we could just give up on social stuff and meet before work here in the shop. Or at Marina's, or, I don't know. Oh God, just tell me what to do."

"All right, I tell you what to do. You meet me for coffee and breakfast and I pay. It's about time, anyway. Eight-thirty?"

"Okay."

Heads turned as Astrid walked into Mister D's Coffee Shop with the same calm presence that she would have shown walking into a classroom, a witness box, or a dress rehearsal. She and Bryce sat in a booth facing one another and gave their orders to Letty.

Bryce grimaced. "So, what did you decide? Am I still part of the plan?"

"Bryce. Please stop. Aren't you our friend? Would we shut you out? Would we treat a friend so badly?"

"Oh, God, I'm sorry. I hate this so much. I hate it that Marina has to face whatever she has to face. I hate it that you're here for the reason you're here for."

"Bryce, we want you to be part of this. Marina loves you, in her way. And it's not a bad thing. It may not be the kind of love that you had hoped for, but you know that it's entirely genuine."

"I understand. And I love Marina. The truth is just that I'm so afraid for her and feel so helpless to do anything."

Astrid looked at the table, sighed, and looked up at him. "I know. I feel the same way."

"Let's start over again. What needs to be done?"

"The doctor called yesterday afternoon with the pathology results. She's a 2B. We don't really know what that means. Marina is researching online everything she can find about breast cancer, which I think may be a bad idea, but I can't stop her. We'll find out for real on Monday when we meet with the oncologist, a Dr. Martini. The jokes about his name must be endless. Marina and I would appreciate it if you could go with us to meet with him. We want you in the exam room, being part of the discussion. Please ask questions and be involved. We'll know a lot more, I think, after that visit, so let's hold off on planning farther ahead than that. We want you to drive, please, and from now on I would like to pay for all the gas and ferry tickets. Please."

"Jesus. I hate this so much."

"I know."

"When is the appointment?"

"We made it for one o'clock, so we could do it in one long day. There's the appointment with Dr. Martini and then another appointment with a nurse for some sort of instruction."

"I'll pick you up at 6:20 tomorrow morning."

Astrid looked at him, and he felt like he had in Paris, that she was a naturalist examining, in the kindliest manner, a curious specimen.

He looked at his watch. "I have to go to work. See you on Monday then," he said.

"Till Monday."

Bryce was almost out the door, when he turned and came back.

"Just let me ask this one question, all right? I need to ask. Do you, does Marina, need money?"

The Astrid smile appeared, with lifted dark eyebrows and the ends of the mouth tucked in at the corner. "I brought a gift to Marina from the family in the form of a nice big check that will keep her going for months. The family has done well in some ways – the restaurant business is thriving - and entrusted me with a reminder of their love and concern. We'll be fine."

Bryce sighed.

Astrid paid at the counter, got on her bicycle, and rode back to Marina's loft. She walked in quietly, but Marina was awake doing range of motion exercises.

"Marina, are you sure you're supposed to be doing all this so soon?"

Marina made a face. "I feel so helpless. What can I do? Nothing. Except exercise. And work. I want to work, but I'm not sure when I'll be strong enough. Massage takes muscle."

"Marina, I just brought you a check that will keep you going very nicely for months. You don't need to rush back to work. Can't you just please rest?"

"That comes so hard! It seems like I'm either exhausted or bored out of my mind. I want to be doing something. How's Bryce?"

"In a way, all three of us are wanting to be doing something we can't do. How's Bryce? Confused and angry, what else? He can help you, he can take you to appointments, he can pick up prescriptions, but he can't fix anything for you. I'm the same way. I'm not so confused, but I am, under this deceptively calm manner, so full of rage. I can't help it. It's how love works."

Marina grinned.

Tall, blonde, and going gray, Dr. Martini walked into the exam room to find two anxious people perched on chairs, and Marina seated cross-legged on the exam table. He stopped in the doorway and smiled at them, his face relaxing into a pleasant maze of wrinkles.

"Hello, all. Maybe we should go to my office," and he led the way to a room with a desk pushed to the wall. There were framed photos of young couples with children on his desk. The windows looked south across the city. On a clear day, he'd have a view of Mt. Rainier. A large framed photo of a river and a stone bridge hung on the wall behind his desk.

They sat on a sofa, he sat at his desk and swiveled to face them.

"Hello, again. I'm Luca Martini. And which of you has the starring role in this production?"

"That would be me. I'm Marina Ollivier."

Bryce and Astrid introduced themselves.

Dr. Martini faced Astrid. "Vous êtes la soeur?" he asked her. His French accent was perfect.

"Pas exactement," she replied. "La tante."

He raised shaggy eyebrows.

"C'est compliqué," she said.

"Chaque famille est compliquée, n'est-ce pas?" He glanced at Bryce and switched to English. "Not as complicated as Marina's next six months are going to be. Let me explain." And he launched into a discussion of what Stage 2B meant, about estrogen-positive receptors, tumor size, lymph-node involvement, and other factors. Dr. Martini went on to describe the series of chemo treatments that Marina would have every two weeks, followed by six weeks of radiation. They questioned and he explained until there were no more questions.

"I know this is all a lot to take in. What I want you to remember is that first of all, Marina, this is a hard year, but you are otherwise in excellent health, and there will be nothing that you can't work through. The second thing is that all we have to go on is numbers; I can only give you statistics, but I assure you that the numbers are strongly on your side. There's every reason to think that you will sail out of this year into a lifetime of good health."

Three bodies visibly relaxed.

Martini stood. "Let's do the exam and then I'll turn you over to the goddess," he said. At Marina's request, Astrid and Bryce accompanied her to the exam room, where Martini confirmed that Marina's healing was going well. As Marina dressed, the doctor shook hands with Bryce and Astrid. He turned, shook hands with Astrid, looked at the three, smiled, and said, "Soyez tranquilles." Bryce's mouth was full of something bitter.

From Dr. Martini's office they went to meet the "goddess," Nurse Katy Bunch. They all sat in Katy's office and she arranged her long arms and legs into a chair next to her desk. Her curly red hair was looped up on her head. She picked up the thick white binder lying on her desk, and presented it to Marina. Inside, like chapters in a book, were sections on chemo, radiation, medication, and more.

"Welcome to Chemo Teach," she said, and went through every section, explaining about each procedure and each prescribed drug, and patiently answering their questions.

"Here's my phone number. Call me! Call me when you have questions and if I don't answer, leave a message and I'll call you back as soon as I can. I'm serious, I mean it – call me! I work Monday through Friday. If you have a question outside that time, call this number. Someone will always answer it or call you back soon. Call us, call us, call us. Got that?"

Marina nodded.

"We'll see you next Wednesday. If you have a question before then, what do you do?"

"Call you?"

"That's the right answer!"

Marina and Astrid and Bryce reeled out of the hospital too tired to think about a restaurant meal. They drove straight to the ferry dock where they barely met the 3:40 sailing. They climbed the stairs up to the galley and found suddenly that they were hungry and thirsty. The ferry galley provided them with beer and burgers, which all three of them attacked enthusiastically, Bryce attempting to stifle his resentment at the annoying Dr. Martini.

Bryce went back to work the next day and for the rest of the day he thought about where he was and what he could do, where he wasn't and what he couldn't do. He didn't know Astrid. It was too much to fantasize about being in love. But if he wasn't in love with Astrid, why was he so annoyed with that kindly-mannered, reassuring, personable, fluent French speaking doctor? Say that somehow he was in love with Astrid. Say even that she loved him (this was completely crazy, he knew), then what? Yes, Astrid was here for a while, maybe a couple of months. Could he imagine that Astrid would leave Paris – and her mother – forever to move to Eliza Island in the San Juan Islands in the Salish Sea? Become an American citizen, perhaps? Could he imagine leaving his life, his business – his family – to live in Paris? What would he do there? Could he live in a tiny apartment and rush out to the park when the sun came out? And what about the language? He could buy a lifetime supply of native speaker level French from the Bookstore of Other Languages. Could he imagine having the $100,000 that would make that possible? If he started taking just regular language classes, how long would it take for him to become fluent enough to make life in Paris imaginable? What was the point of all this imagining, anyway? He had no clues from her about how she felt about him beyond friendship heightened by the situation they now found themselves in. What was he thinking?

He had no one to talk with. He couldn't bring himself to submit the question to the Friday Study Group. He didn't sleep well, but no midnight conversations with himself brought any clarity. What to do? What to do?

On Wednesday, they went in for Marina's first chemo session. Bryce had come to a conclusion about his course of action, but he couldn't leave Marina and Astrid for the first chemo session. It would have to be next time. Marina went in for a blood test and then returned to the tasteful waiting room, where they all sat leafing through magazines. At last Katy Bunch came for them and led them into a small room painted a cheerful soft yellow.

Katy sat Marina in a padded, reclining chair and chatted with her while she connected an IV to her port. "I'll stay with you for a bit, but you should be fine." She sat next to Marina and chatted with her about a brochure on wigs and scarves and cosmetics, and all the time observing her. After about twenty minutes, she asked if Marina needed anything and Marina said no. "This is a call button," Katy added "in case you should have a question. This is a panic button; push it and somebody will be here before you let up on the button!"

The afternoon ticked along. Marina had brought her tablet, and checked in with her Facebook friends around the world, and then turned to the e-book she was reading. Astrid wrote a long letter to her mother, then turned to her book, a new biography of Coco Chanel. Bryce stayed with them, read Wolf Hall, and thought about how he was going to escape during the next session, two weeks later.

From time to time Astrid or Bryce would examine Marina cautiously. She finally caught them scrutinizing her. "I'm not going to burst into flames, you know!" They quickly turned their attention back to their books.

There was a tap on the door, and Dr. Martini looked in. "Bon jour!" Marina nodded, "Bonjour! Entrez!"

"Tout va bien? he asked. Vous avez des questions?" and Dr. Martini and Marina spent several minutes in conversation before he remembered that one of the group was being left out.

"Anybody else have any questions?" he asked, looking at Bryce. Bryce shook his head and clenched his jaw, and the doctor said his adieux and went on to the next patient.

After a couple of hours it was all over. Katy came in, freed Marina from her IV, and put a Bugs Bunny band-aid over her port. They packed up their things and walked to the parking garage, and drove home.

The next day, Thursday, Marina felt fine, and went into the clinic for a white blood cell booster shot. On Thursday evening she said she felt a little slow, and on Friday she was flat on her back.

"I've never had a fatigue like this," she said to Astrid. "It's not like I'm sleepy and it's not being tired in any way that I've ever experienced. It's like somebody opened a spigot and let it run and I'm out of whatever it takes to sit up or think. And the nausea is different, too. It's not like I really feel like I'm going to vomit. It's more that I feel like I'm suspended in a bottle of formaldehyde. It's just an all-encompassing universal ickiness."

Astrid chose from an array of amber plastic bottles, and offered one to Marina. "Try one of these."

On Saturday it was the same. Marina spent the day almost motionless, listening to an audio book. On Sunday noon, it lifted almost as quickly as it had come on. "Just like a heavy blanket that's been covering me, and somebody slowly lifts it off," she said. On Sunday afternoon she got up, took a shower, and on Monday she was well enough to take Astrid on a tour of the local history museum. Astrid came back eager to know more about the Central Coast Salish Tribes, salmon, smallpox, and the Spanish explorer, Francisco Eliza.

Life resumed. On the evening before Marina's next treatment, she and Astrid invited Bryce to dinner in their loft above the chandlery. The simple dinner of manicotti and salad and baguette became a European feast. Astrid and Bryce drank most of the bottle of Beaujolais, with Marina taking only a taste.

"I've never been very interested in being pure," she said, "but, hey they're the only two kidneys I have and they're being stressed enough."

Bryce raised his glass: "To Marina's purity!" and Astrid responded: "And to its early demise!"

Marina brightened. "Thank you! The sooner the better!"

Bryce said, "Hey, Marina. I'm trying, I really am, not to hover over you, but how about an update?"

"Okay, okay. Really, I mostly feel fine. From what I hear and read online, this is the pattern: treatment, crash, then back on your feet. There is one thing that bothers me, though, and it's kind of embarrassing to admit."

"Yes? Yes?"

"It's been almost two weeks since my first treatment. Why hasn't my hair fallen out?"

"What do you think?" asked Bryce. "You think they're firing blanks at you?"

Marina smiled. "I told you it was embarrassing."

"How about I give you a haircut?" asked Astrid. "Then when it falls out, there will be less to fall out."

"Not when you've just drunk a half a bottle of wine."

"We could do something very experimental," said Astrid seductively.

"Oh, sure. Why not? I have – literally – nothing to lose. I'm going to lose it anyway."

Astrid walked Bryce to the stairs. "What a good friend you are," she said.

Bryce shook his head. "I'm a friend to Marina, and she's the one I've slept with. I don't know what I am to you."

Astrid's smile disappeared and she looked him in the eye. "We are friends," she said.

She looked at him in her examining way, curious, slightly worried. She held him in her gaze for a full minute.

"Good night."

The next day, Bryce called Linda.

"Hi, Mom."

"Bryce! How are you?"

"Oh, I'm fine, Mom, but I have a question."

"Yes?"

"I want to make dinner for a friend who is having chemo. What can I make that's kind of bland, but makes me look like a great cook?"

"Hmmm. Summer. How about a nice cool salad? You could marinate some red onion slices – would that be too much? Would tuna be okay? Kalamata olives? Hard-boiled eggs? Look up Salad Niçoise."

"Mom, you are a life-saver!"

"Who is she?"

"Thanks, Mom! Talk to you later!"

Bryce picked them up early Wednesday morning, his plan in place. Marina's long black tresses were gone, replaced by a near crew cut and asymmetric bangs. He wanted to weep.

In Seattle, they parked at the hospital, went in, and Marina checked in at the desk. Bryce accompanied them to Hematology and waited until Katy had Marina hooked up to the poison-delivering device.

"I thought today I might go for a walk today," he said casually. Marina and Astrid looked up, a little surprised, but nodded. "Good idea," said Marina.

He left the hospital feeling a little furtive, but determined nonetheless. He hailed a cab and gave the address of The Bookstore of Other Languages. He opened the door, and looked around. In the back of the store, Cilla and Dr. Milton were standing in front of the office door, deep in conversation. Cilla glanced at Bryce and quickly moved away, frowning. Milton shrugged and went in his office and closed the door.

Cilla greeted him. "Mr. Hanford! I saw that you have an appointment today. French this time!"

"Right. French."

"How much do you need?"

"I need three months at tourist level."

"That's wonderful! Are you traveling all that time?"

Bryce frowned. "My plans aren't really in place yet."

Cilla took a step back. "Oh. I'm sorry. I didn't mean to be nosy. Well then, at $300 per week, that would be $3600, but if you buy a whole quarter we discount it to $3,000."

Bryce handed over his credit card. He had moved money from his savings account into his checking account, making a substantial dent.

"I do have a question, though."

"Yes?"

"When I was in Albania, I hardly realized that I was speaking, reading, and understanding Albanian. It just happened. When I was in France, it was easier. But now, I'm going to be right here and sometimes I'll want to speak English, most of the time, just like I ordinarily do, but then sometimes I'll want to use French."

"Oh, that's not a problem. You'll understand both English and French and you'll speak whichever you choose. You know, you won't even need to choose – even people who have grown up speaking more than one language respond to cues from other people or situations. It won't be a problem for you."

After his treatment – so much easier than Marina's, he walked uphill back to the hospital with the familiar faint head-ache and got there just as Marina was finishing.

"Where have you been?" Marina asked.

"Ne me pose pas la question," he answered and two pairs of eyebrows raised, two mouths pursed.

Already Bryce felt that his money was well-spent.

REPORT: TMS

HANFORD, BRYCE, CLIENT #0022

LANGUAGE, LEVEL OF PROFICIENCY, DURATION, PRICE:

FRENCH, TOURIST, ONE QUARTER: $3,000

TECHNICIAN: CILLA M.

REASON FOR CONTACT AND PROGNOSIS FOR FUTURE EN-GAGEMENT:

This is Mr. Hanford's third session. He refused to talk about his reason for making this substantial purchase, and he seemed very tense. Questionable prognosis for future engagement, although the client's urgency suggests a serious need.

CHAPTER SEVEN

Bryce and Astrid and Marina came to an understanding that
from now on they would speak French among themselves and
English in front of others. Bryce felt embarrassed, but refused
to divulge the secret of his sudden fluency. If their curiosity
remained unsatisfied, the two women agreed not to tease him
about it. And besides, they had more pressing problems to
solve.

Not long after the second treatment Marina quit speculating
about whether or not the chemotherapy was working. Her
small bits of remaining hair came off in her hairbrush and fell
on her clothes. She had to put in a screen at the bottom of her
shower to catch the wisps. Marina and Astrid looked at wigs
online, arguing over which would be best. Would it be better
to get short straight black hair so that when her own hair grew
back in it wouldn't be so different? Or was this the opportunity
to be a blonde or a redhead, to have curly hair for once in her
life? Or would it be better just to be bald and wear lots of
makeup and huge earrings? These questions occupied them

until the next treatment, when they asked Bryce if he would take them to a wig store outside of Seattle.

Unwilling and unable to participate in so intensely feminine an event, Bryce told them to take their time, but that he would wait in the car. After forty minutes they emerged, Astrid as always, Marina with loose auburn curls that fell around her neck and hid any trace of the edge of the wig. Her blue eyes were startling as she grinned at him.

That evening, Bryce looked around his house, wondering what it would look like to Astrid and Marina. Yes, it was plumbed and wired and insulated, but how did it look? He remembered Astrid's apartment, with its African quilts and ficus in a ceramic tub. He thought his living room looked a little bleak. Just as well it was August. They could eat on the deck, where you could see the garden, lush with vegetables, then over the treetops, and to the water beyond.

They came and, to Bryce's relief, exclaimed over the view, and settled happily into cushioned deck chairs. He had made sangria for himself and Astrid, and had made a drink for Marina of lemonade, carbonated water, and mint leaves.

"You have to use as much mint as possible," he explained. "Otherwise it will overrun the Island."

Astrid smiled at him. "Bryce, I am very curious about something," she began. "Marina took me to the little historical museum here, and I want to know more about the Coast Salish tribes and Francisco Eliza and smallpox, and all about the history of the Island."

"It's a little embarrassing to have been reading about European history and knowing so little about the history here," he replied. But he offered what he could remember about Lushootseed culture and the sorry history of Anglo conquest.

"One thing I've always meant to do was to go look at some of the petroglyphs. Some of them have been photographed, but they won't tell you where they are – understandably. But you can visit others."

"I've seen cave paintings in the Dordogne," Astrid answered. "You think they're going to look old and dusty, but they looked so fresh, and you think you might know the artist."

Bryce brought out his salad, built up like architecture with potatoes, red onion slices, asparagus, and roasted red sweet peppers, almost all fresh from his garden. With grilled fish and store-bought French bread, it was a feast that lasted until after the late summer sun set.

At the fifth chemo session, at the beginning of September, Katy Bunch sat with Marina a little while longer.

"Marina, I bet you remember every word of that Chemo Teach we did a few weeks ago, yes?"

"Right. Or maybe not. Do you know I think I really do have chemo brain. I take longer to figure things out. I get confused easily."

"Marina, you are handling more than anybody was ever meant to handle. Something has to give. Believe me, it will all come back. In the meantime, be good to yourself, yes? Repeat morning, noon, and night 'I am a goddess, I am invincible.'"

"Sounds good! I like that!"

"Say it!"

"I am a goddess! I am invincible!"

"Good!" Katy pushed her long curly pony tail aside. "What I want to remind you of is that today we start a new drug. You're done with half of the series, and in most people's opinion, you're over the hardest part."

"This is sounding even better." Marina looked suspiciously at Katy. "Can I trust you? What do you have up your sleeve? Up my sleeve? Up my port?"

Katy smiled. "The best thing about this one is that it doesn't have the feeling that you describe as universal ickiness."

"Thank God for small favors."

"You'll still have the fatigue, just like you do now, and most people experience a fair amount of joint pain. And *some* people experience a serious amount of joint pain. You have a list of side effects in your binder – it's a whole page long. So today you and I are going to have a little chat about pain management."

"Did I say something about small favors? It's true – modern medicine is full of miracles. Look at me – I'm alive. But I have to say the miracles are a little hard on the patient."

Katy looked serious for a minute. "I know. I've been there."

Astrid and Bryce swiveled their heads.

"Really?" asked Marina.

Katy pointed at her left breast. "See this? Came from Nordstrom. Really. Marina, here's the truth. You can't tell by looking who has shared this experience with you. It's a great big sisterhood. You'll see. In the meantime - you are a goddess. You are invincible. And you are not alone. Now let's talk pain management." And they did. When they were finished, Katy gave Marina a new prescription, kissed her on the cheek, and left.

In the galley of the ferry, Astrid and Bryce got beers, Marina got ice tea, and they slumped into their seats. Marina moped.

"It's so unfair. It's actually not that hard to give up alcohol, because I don't really want it. I miss it, but then when I think about it I don't want it. What's unfair is that I don't want coffee, either. I've been having steamed milk with almond flavoring. What has life come to that I don't want either wine or coffee? This is not life as we know it."

Astrid raised her eyebrows. "This is why we're supposed to feel sorry for you?"

"Come to think of it, yes. Yes, feel sorry for me for that and the rest is just life. Be glad I can be cured and be sorry that I drink steamed milk."

"Je suis tellement désolée pour toi, chérie."

"Ça ne m'interesse pas!"

Astrid smiled at her, and then the smile went away. She looked at them both and became serious.

"My dears, I have something difficult to talk with you about."

"I'm not going to like this," said Marina. "I know I'm not."

"That's right, you're not. Marina. Bryce. I have to go home. I have to go back to France. Mama is fed up with Brittany and Oncle Yves and Tante Juliette are fed up with her. Also, the school year is starting and I have to start work."

Nobody wanted to say anything. Nobody liked it, nobody could argue. In silence they went back to the car and drove off the ferry. Bryce took them to the chandlery, and they sat silently in the car.

"Are you going to forgive me?" asked Astrid.

"How can you ask?" answered Marina. You've saved my life. I can do the rest – with Bryce's help."

"No," said Bryce, thinking he might never see her again.

Bryce continued to take Marina to her appointments. Katy continued to attend Marina as a minor goddess attends a major goddess. Dr. Martini visited Marina each time, chatting pleasantly in French, engaging Bryce, although clearly a little skeptical about his sudden fluency. Martini followed Marina's progress, looked carefully over her labs, asking questions, and answering her questions. He was sorry to hear that Astrid had gone back to France and sent her his best wishes.

Bryce tried to shake off the painful sense of loss. The Friday Study Group became delicate, offering him an opportunity to tell them about his situation, but being quick to turn the conversation to the latest faculty gossip, the most recent irresponsible City Council decision, the collapse of Kurt's weekend dojo.

He turned his mind to work. Justin and Kendra had had to take over some of his work, but when Bryce assessed the current situation he found that his employees were reliable and skilled, his customers trusted them, and that new business opportunities continued to present themselves, in particular a local real estate office that had expanded, adding three new sales people and moving into a new building. It was a good thing, he thought, that Justin's and Kendra's skills were so complementary. Also, they seemed to get along well, which was a good thing.

Marina's last chemo session was coming soon. Radiation treatments were five days a week for six weeks and Dr. Martini told her that when people lived as far away from the hospital as she did, they often find a way to move to Seattle for six weeks. In her case, though, a new radiation clinic had opened on the mainland, in Anacortes, where the ferry docked. "I know the partners in the clinic – they're former colleagues here – and I know that they are very good in their specialties. You'd still be on two ferries, but then you'd be spared the drive into Seattle. It's even within walking distance of the ferry dock."

At the last chemo session Bryce took a moment with the doctor in the waiting room while Marina was having her blood taken. "Can you tell me anything? Marina is, as you said earlier, the star in the production, but for those of us in supporting roles, it's hard, too. I just have some questions."

Dr. Martini's smile maze appeared. "You and Astrid have been marvelous. I do know it's hard. You're about done with the practical help now, and in a way, that's harder. Marina will be able to go to radiation on her own. Your role is subtler, but it's still there. Encourage her to get regular moderate exercise, for example."

"Oh, don't worry about that."

"You're right. I have gotten to know Marina a little over the last few months."

"Tell me truly. How bad is radiation?"

"It doesn't hurt. Really. The first time it does hurt because the patient has to stay in a difficult position while the techs measure all kinds of things. Radiation is very specific – we don't want to hit her lungs or heart."

"Jesus!"

"Bryce, I know it sounds scary, and I'm not saying that no radiation specialist has ever made a mistake, but really, it's very rare, and radiation really helps. We've done the cutting and poisoning part. Now it's time for the burning."

Bryce shook his head. "You'd think that one or two treatments like that would do it? Why so much?"

Dr. Martini shrugged and lifted his white eyebrows. "After the surgeon takes out the tumor, we can't see anything, and we don't know what might be left over. Chemo is systemic. The poison goes all through the body, killing any cells that might be traveling around looking for a place to settle down. Radiation is local. It focuses on the place the tumor was and gives it hell."

"I keep telling myself that Marina is being treated with miracles of modern medicine, but anybody can see it's wearing her down."

"Marina is a healthy, strong, young woman. I hate seeing young women hit with this – well, truly, I hate seeing anybody hit with it – but she will be fine. I always have to back off and say that there are occasions when somebody doesn't make it, but everything is in her favor! Maybe you're the one who needs to repeat Katy's mantra: Marina is a goddess; Marina is invincible."

"Last chemo! Yay!"

"Last chemo! Yay!"

They drove up the freeway cheering, and at one point Marina opened up and screamed one long joyous scream.

On the ferry they went upstairs to sit by the windows and watch the sun set on the islands.

Marina took his hand.

"Bryce. You good, good friend."

He patted her hand.

"Let me buy you dinner?"

He thought a minute. "Let's make a deal. You take me out to dinner tonight and I take you out to dinner in a week or two, when you feel like drinking a glass of wine."

"Deal! Where do you want to go?"

"You choose."

"Let's go to the Crab Pot and get chowder. It actually sounds good."

A few local heads turned when they walked into the Crab Pot. Sarina, the waitress, smiled at Marina and led them to a table by a window. A strange silence descended on the loud and lively pub. People looked at Marina and smiled. Then, as if they had rehearsed it, everyone stood and cheered, whistled and stamped their feet.

Sarina, still smiling, said, "It's on the house tonight, folks! What'll it be?" They ordered clam chowder, a beer for Bryce and an herbal tea for Marina. As they ate, people came up to their table, laid a hand on Marina's shoulder or bent over and gave her a kiss.

Marina leaned over the table and whispered to Bryce, "Did you plan this?"

"No! How could I? You suggested going out. You picked the place."

"What happened?"

"It's a small town. Everybody knows everything, and they're happy you're through with chemo. People love you." He lowered his voice to a threatening growl, "Deal with it, Baby!"

Marina grinned, her blue eyes gleamed, her expensive synthetic auburn curls shimmered in the fake candlelight.

After one more weekend of deep fatigue and aching joints she was well and truly done with chemo and had earned two weeks of rest.

Before she started radiation Bryce suggested an expedition. "How about we go island-hopping and have paella at La Valenciana? Complete with wine for a change?"

They stretched out the long September evening, enjoying the rich seafoods and saffron rice of the paella, sipping their way through a bottle of Spanish rioja. They walked out of the restaurant into a night still warm, but with a dark island sky. On the ferry home they stood alone on the deck, lost in the black sky, sequined with stars and mirrored by the dark rippling Salish Sea. They leaned over the railing and Marina put her arm around Bryce's waist. He put his arm around her shoulder and pulled her closer.

They drove back to her loft at the chandlery and Bryce turned off the car.

"Come upstairs with me," she whispered. "I'm afraid, but come up with me anyway."

"You're never afraid," he whispered back, "but I'll come anyway."

"You're right. I'm not afraid."

In the loft, she didn't turn the light on, but reached out her arms to him, and he kissed her, careful not to put pressure on the wounded side.

"Don't worry," she said, "I'm healed."

Yes, he thought, later that night, holding her in his arms. Yes, you are healed.

E-mail from Marina to Astrid:

I have to tell you what happened. Ugh. I don't mean ugh about what happened, I mean ugh about telling you. I am feeling so much better, and Bryce took me out to celebrate and, as they say, always so lamely, one thing led to another, and that thing led to the other thing, which was my bed. I think I'm just going to tell you that and then run away.

Write me if you forgive me.

Marina

The next morning Bryce left his car at home and walked three miles to work. He had a lot to sort out and told himself that he had no idea where to begin. Then he realized that he did know where to begin, though, and that was with the pleasures of last night. He found himself falling back on the cliché that though he loved Marina – he did love her! – he was not in love with her. Then he asked himself, what difference it made? If you loved someone and if your bodies found one another with ease and joy, what difference did it make? But then he came up with the distressing answer that it made a huge difference when that person was brave, exultant, footloose Marina. What he wanted was the feeling of those hours in Paris, talking with Astrid openly, the way he yearned and ached for, and it was not reasonable to find yourself yearning and aching for conversation the way one yearned and ached for sex. Conversation with Astrid was, well, it was not sexy, exactly, but it involved a union of sorts, not that they agreed on anything in particular, except there was a foundation. Of what? Of trust? An agreement of what was worth talking about? Or was it just Astrid's manner? Her calm presence under which ran streams of sly, stealthy humor? Her air of benign scrutiny that gave him the sense that she wanted to see him for who he was, that she wanted to know the best of him but would not shy from knowing the whole truth about him, whatever it was? The acceptance that made him feel as if he were in some unexplored country, and that felt, at the same time, like a home he had never known. By the time he arrived at work he had been unable to see any way forward.

E-mail from Astrid to Marina:

Oh, Marina, my feelings are such a mess. How can I be mad at you? I own no one; I have no claims on Bryce. I can do nothing but wish myself in your place. Do I like it? No, in my heart's heart I do not, but it is helpless jealousy on my part. I think maybe what would be best is if you tell me nothing more.

Do tell me, though, how the radiation is going.

Love,

Astrid

E-mail from Marina to Astrid:

When I grow up can I be like you? Really though, you do un-
derstand that I think you are totally crazy, loco, verrückt? What is
wrong with you? Damn it, you take things so seriously! Forget that
asshole from the past, and won't you please give yourself a
chance? And I know you told me not to tell you anymore, but I will
just add a report from the battlefront that you have nothing to
fear from Bryce. Really. Nothing at all.

And in other news, my radiation is coming along nicely. I go in
for treatments every day and meet with Dr. Gupta, a very pleasant
woman from New Delhi, who examines my chest with the air of a
woman inspecting a roast beef in the oven, although come to think
of it, she's probably Hindu, so I wouldn't be roast beef, but more
likely roast pork. She says I'm coming along nicely, so in a couple
of weeks I'll be ready to be served up. Do Hindus serve roast pig
with an apple in its mouth?

Also, my hair is coming in and amazingly, it is curly! I've al-
ways envied women with curly hair and now I have it, although
people say it won't last. It is incredibly fine and soft. I'd give up my
wig for good if it hadn't turned chilly here – darker, too! – and my
head gets cold without it.

Grateful love always,

Marina

After Marina was through with radiation, she and Bryce made
one more trip to the hospital to check in with Dr. Martini.

"You're done with the hard part," he said, with his familiar warm smile.

"There's more?"

"We want to see you every three months for the next two years, and we need to stay in touch about the hormone therapy you'll be taking."

Marina looked over at Bryce, sitting against the wall.

"Bryce, I haven't talked this over with you, and I haven't mentioned it to you, either, Doctor, but it's getting cold and dark here. It's time for me to take off."

"Where?" asked Dr. Martini.

Bryce was speechless.

"Last year I went to Sydney and I thought I'd go there again. There a job for me there, and it's spring. Surely they have hospitals in Australia where I can be checked out."

Doctor Martini sighed. "I don't like it, but yes, I can't stop you. Will you be coming back here? If so, when?"

"I could come back here in the spring. I can always find a job here."

"If you come back in the spring you can arrange it so that you'd only miss one appointment here. You will be sure to check with someone in Australia at three months out, won't you? Let me know where you are and I'll find the nearest and best place."

Marina grinned. "You got a deal!"

Bryce glared at Marina. "You are heartless!"

She twisted around inside her seat belt.

"I am not! You know me, what did you think? I was going to change? What were you thinking? What *were* you thinking?"

"God only knows!"

"Bryce! Did you think I was going to be so grateful to you for all your help that I was going to" – she threw her eyes to heaven – "change my ways and be" – she pouted and sniffed theatrically – "yours forever?"

"That is a mean and heartless thing to say. What did YOU think I was doing? Buying you mile by mile?"

"Bryce, stop it!"

He drove on in silence, then erupted again.

"You and your aunt are both heartless and I hope to God I never see either of you again."

She said nothing, and they drove on.

On the last ferry Marina came to a difficult conclusion.

"Bryce, I want us to stay in the car. There's something I need to tell you."

He looked at her sourly.

"I want to tell you about Astrid."

"Astrid can go to hell. She and her mother and Oncle Yves and Tante Juliette and Mme. Mercier and the entire Fourteenth Arrondissement can go to hell for all I care."

"Listen, Bryce! Behave yourself! I'm being serious!"

Marina looked straight at him. She *was* serious. It was unsettling.

"What?"

"Look, this should be no big deal, not really, but it is to Astrid, and she'll shoot me for telling you."

Bryce knew that he should be stopping her but he couldn't speak.

"Four years ago Astrid had breast cancer and was really sick with the chemo and other treatment, plus she lost a breast. So Jean-Michel, her asshole husband, whom none of us liked, ever, got bored and left her. I mean, really, if it were me, I'd just have kicked him out on his ass and found somebody else. Life is too short to go around wringing your hands all the time and moaning about mean bastards. Fuck 'em. Anyway, she's fine now, she's healthy, her hair grew back, she's as gorgeous as ever. Yeah, she lost a breast, but that only means she doesn't have to deal with selfish bastards. But you know Astrid – she lives so deep inside herself. So she sits around guarding her precious secret and living with her mother. She would never tell you, but I'm sure that's what's holding her back."

Bryce sat back in his seat and stared into space.

Marina got impatient. "So that's her big secret."

The ferry docked and the people at the front started their cars.

Marina rolled her eyes.

"You're in love with her."

"I don't know. Being with her was so different, it was another world."

"Well, duh, it is another world. You met her in Paris. There's a reason why every tourist and his brother wants to go to Paris, right? I'm so sorry I ever suggested it. You should have gone to Rio or Acapulco or someplace not so deadly serious."

"No, it wouldn't have mattered where I went. I mean, it mattered enormously that I went to Paris because I met Astrid, but I would have been serious anywhere. Send me to Vegas and I'd still be serious."

She shrugged. "And since I'm blabbing, I'll tell you her other big secret – she's in love with you. Or at least I'm pretty sure she is. That's all I have to say. I'm packing up and taking off. Nice knowing you. See you in May. If you don't go back to Paris and beat Astrid's door down, you're crazy."

"I don't think I can."

E-mail from Marina to Astrid:

I told him. So shoot me.

Marina

CHAPTER EIGHT

Bryce put his head down and focused on business. Fall had come, and the holiday inventory was already arriving. While the Island population had its share of artists who scraped by on sales to summer tourists, it had also had affluent year-rounders, drawn by the spectacular views, relatively temperate weather and, in some cases, the privacy, at least from the mainland – Eliza Island had a few reclusive celebrities. The Island had its old Subarus and its brand-new BMWs; its old Kias and its new Land Rovers, but everybody knew about everybody else or at least knew someone else who knew them. They all shopped at Hanford Computers, Etc.

The community was affluent enough to support local businesses, and the population was too small to attract the big box stores. Thus, Bryce was able to stock his shop with a substantial range of the latest computers, phones, tablets, toys, and devices, knowing that most of his customers would come to him before they ordered online. They wanted to talk over their purchases with him, they trusted his advice, and it was a community that realized that without local businesses, life would be very different. As the holidays approached, they came and they bought. Things were so busy that Bryce hired Taylor, a high school student, to wrap presents. Finally, at four o'clock on the afternoon of December 24th, they locked the door and looked at one another with relief.

"Done!" said Bryce. He gave envelopes with checks inside to Justin, Kendra, and Taylor, wished them well, and waved good-bye to them as they left into the dark, drizzly afternoon. Just a few more last chores and he'd be ready to go home. He sat at his computer.

Someone tapped on the glass door, and there were Justin and Kendra. What had gone wrong? He opened the door.

"Uh, Bryce?" said Kendra.

"Yeah . . . that would be me."

"Well, we wanted to thank you for the checks. They're great!"

"You're welcome." Bryce shrugged. "In spite of all the drama of the year, we've done great business. You two have made that possible. While I was dividing my year between France and the oncology department, you guys were working."

Justin looked a little sheepish. "Uh, could we take you out for an early beer?"

Bryce looked at them suspiciously. "Why not?" and they headed for the Crab Pot.

The Crab Pot was full of local merchants who had turned off their computers and their lights, and locked up their stores. The holiday rush was over, and it was time to celebrate. Bryce and Justin and Kendra got their beers and eased their way through the crowd to the last open table. They hung up their parkas, brushed the rain off their faces, and sat. Justin and Kendra stared at Bryce.

"What? What is going on?"

"It's about the checks," said Justin.

"What about them?"

"Oh, just tell him, Justin!" said Kendra, smiling and flipping her braids behind her.

"We're using the checks to go on our honeymoon. We're getting married in February and going to Hawaii for our honeymoon."

In the long drive south on Christmas morning, Bryce tried to feel nothing but pleasure for Justin and Kendra. He did not want to think of himself as someone who felt sorry for himself when others were happy. He didn't want to grudge them their blissful smiles or their relief at announcing to him, as if to the world, that everything was suddenly new, that they were in love, that they were going to live happily ever after. He wound up thinking poorly of himself, of having failed to be that other finer, better person. He went on then to think poorly of himself for judging himself so harshly, and finally arrived at his parents' house very much in need of cheering up. It was snowing when he got out of the car and opened the trunk to pull out his backpack and a large bag of wrapped presents.

Sally and Kenny were already there, with Cole and Connor. While they and Roger and Linda were greeting Bryce, Uncle Mel drove up. Roger and Linda had announced several years ago that they were both sick and tired of turkey and they hoped never to cook another. Their Christmas dinner was a salmon surrounded by mushroom slices covered with tarragon cream, wild rice with onions, walnuts, and celery, a salad, and the one concession to the conventional holiday table, gingered yams. Sally was the pie baker and had brought apple and mincemeat. Santa had come that morning for the boys, so they were able to sit at the dinner table – prudently separated by Sally - and wait for the present exchange with only moderate antsiness.

Against his will, Bryce asked Uncle Mel about Brenda.

"Bryce, I don't know. I think she's in the Adriatic again."

"No. Just no. Not in Albania, I hope," said Bryce.

"I know nothing. She's stopped e-mailing me, but I've given up worrying about her. I mean, I do worry, but I realize she's not going to keep in touch." Mel sighed. "She's too much for me. Linda, could I have a bit more salmon?"

Dinner over, presents were given and received. Bryce gave modest, but newly released, computer games to each of the boys. Sally's rule, made when the boys were very young, was that everyone who received a present gave a present. Bryce looked forward each year to his gifts. This year Connor gave him a laminated guide to shore birds of the Pacific Northwest; Cole had made him a picture of a great blue heron. Bryce pronounced himself to be more pleased by these gifts than by anything Santa could have brought him. Santa knew nothing! Connor and Cole knew what he had been wanting!

Later, they packed the children in the car and drove to see the ZooLights. At the Oregon Zoo, they walked around in the dark night marveling at the million-and-a-half colored lights in the shapes of alligators and giraffes, hippos and flamingoes.

They got back home at ten, the boys having fallen asleep in the car. Christmas was over.

E-mail from Marina to Astrid:

Dear One,

It's Christmas in Sydney, warm and sunny. I went to a glass-blowing demonstration, then had drinks with friends and came back to the apartment and sat and thought. This just isn't working. I think I'm getting old, Astrid. I don't know if it's the cancer or that I'm in my thirties now, but I'm missing home. I want to come back. I want to be with family, with Mama and Papa. I want to see you and Aunt Thérèse. Where are you now? Paris or Brittany? Can I use the apartment?

I had my check-up and I'm fine. They said they'd tell Dr. Martini.

Love always,

Marina

E-mail from Astrid to Marina:

Uncle Yves and Aunt Juliette are here in Paris in the apartment. They are dying to see you. Come home. You can stay with Mama and me. There's always a place for you.

Merry Christmas!

Astrid

Justin and Kendra and Bryce worked hard in those two weeks after Christmas. In spite of having put up signs carefully describing the conditions under which they would allow customers to return merchandise, they were forced to deal with people who thought the shop should take back a tablet that had been beaten on the floor by a toddler or a phone that had gone through the wash. That was the worst. Most of the people were merely frustrated or confused by new technology. With much patience and skill, problems were solved and most customers satisfied. In the end there did turn out to be one sad exception.

"I completely understand, Mrs. Schroeder, and I'm so sorry for your loss," said Bryce, putting the dog activity monitor back into inventory and refunding Mrs. Schroeder's money. Her Christmas present to Fritzi had come too late.

Early one morning, Bryce woke to a sudden blast of Merle Haggard singing "Mama Tried," and reached for his phone.

"Mom! Are you okay?"

"Oh, dear, Bryce, I've woken you up. I'm so sorry, but we are in a mess here."

"What?"

"Are you sitting down?"

"Mom, I'm in bed!"

"It's Brenda."

"No, goddamnit, no, no no!"

"Well, but yes, and Uncle Mel doesn't know what to do."

"Let her rot in Mongolia or Peru or wherever the hell she's stuck now."

Linda sighed.

"Albania."

Bryce closed his eyes.

"Mom, I'm hanging up." And he did.

As he expected, Merle Haggard announced a return call from Linda.

"Bryce, don't be rude."

"I'm not being rude to you, Mom, I'm saying that I have done my duty by Brenda and somebody else can do it now. Why me?"

"Why you is because there is nobody else. Will you listen to me?"

"No! Oh, okay. Yes."

"She needs $37,000 in cash or she can't get out of the country."

"Why on God's green earth does she need $37,000?"

"She can't tell us."

"Can I even take that much cash out of the country?"

"Is there someone you can ask?"

"I'll look it up online."

"Oh, good! Does that mean you'll do it?"

"NO!"

"Shall I tell Uncle Mel that you won't do it?"

Bryce hung up and cursed heartily for a full minute, then called his mother.

"Okay," he said. "Where is she?"

"She has a suite at the Polaris Tirana Hotel. She says she'll have a bed brought in for you."

"What a gal."

"She says to hurry, she's being pressured. We can't imagine what's going on, but it's very scary. She said she'll pay you back for everything, and you know she is always very good about money."

"Money is where Brenda lives. Talk to you later, Mom."

Bryce hung up for the third time and thought it over. He called Justin. He looked at the phone and thought carefully. This time he'd be better prepared. Time to talk with Stevie.

Bryce texted to the number Stevie had given him and a few minutes later his phone rang.

"Stevie here. What's happening, Bryce?"

Bryce told Stevie what he had learned from Linda. Stevie was silent for a moment, then spoke.

"All right, Bryce. I'm pretty sure I know what's going on and who she's dealing with. She must have run out of money. These people deal in much bigger sums than $37,000."

"Stevie, I have no idea."

"No. And it's a good thing you don't. It's really nothing anybody wants to be involved with."

"Except, apparently, Brenda."

"As you say."

"Also, Stevie. This is going to sound really weird. Maybe you won't believe me, but for the next week, I'll be speaking Albanian."

There was silence.

"Bryce, I don't have a lot of time. Can you explain quickly?"

"I don't think so. There's a place in Seattle where you can buy language fluency. They kind of insert it in your head. I know you're not going to believe this."

Silence again.

"We'll talk more about this. You'll be able to understand these people?"

"Yes."

"Will they know you can understand them?"

"Not if I don't tell them."

"Don't. You leave this evening?"

"Right."

"I'm going to make a couple of calls. I'll be back to you within the hour."

"I'll be here."

Bryce showered and dressed and was eating breakfast when Stevie called back.

"Okay, here's what you do." And Stevie gave Bryce a minimal description of what was going on and then gave his instructions.

REPORT: TMS

HANFORD, BRYCE, CLIENT #0022

LANGUAGE, LEVEL OF PROFICIENCY, DURATION, PRICE:

ALBANIAN, BUSINESS, ONE WEEK: $500

TECHNICIAN: CILLA M.

REASON FOR CONTACT AND PROGNOSIS FOR FUTURE ENGAGEMENT:

This is Mr. Hanford's fourth session. Prognosis for future engagement seems more likely than not, as a fourth visit correlates very strongly with continued patronage, although his visits have not been typical of our clientele's general interest in language for tourism or business. We don't usually get that many customers coming for Albanian!

After a full day of travel, Bryce arrived in Tirana. He negotiated the same checkpoints that he had gone through the year
before, retrieved his luggage, patted his money belt and other
places where he had concealed a great deal of cash, and walked
to the rent-a-phone counter, where he supplied himself with a
cell phone and immediately made a call; a severe voice answered and Bryce asked for Stevie. After a short wait, Stevie
assured him that all was ready. Bryce gave his new phone
number to Stevie, and went over the plan again. When he
hung up he felt far more confident. This time he had a Higher
Power watching over him. And unlike the last time he was
here, he was aware that he was speaking fluent Albanian. He
took his backpack outside and got into a cab.

At the Polaris Tirana Hotel reception desk, he asked for
Brenda Bongiorno, and was connected to her room.

"God, you're late. Come up here!"

He arrived at her room, knocked, and the door was opened
by a heavy-browed, shaven-headed man who looked like an
Olympic wrestler. He wore a Reed College sweatshirt ("Com-
munism, Atheism, Free Love"), jeans, and running shoes. The
wrestler made room for Bryce to come in. Brenda, one ankle
wrapped in a bandage, was seated next to a table littered with
the remains of three breakfasts. Two aluminum crutches were
parked against her chair. Standing next to her was a long-jawed
man with a stubble beard, dressed in a smartly-tailored suit.

Bryce looked at the crutches. "What have you done this
time?" he asked.

"What do you think? I tripped on one of their goddamn
sidewalks again and sprained an ankle. Nothing like last time."

"Bryce," Brenda continued, indicating the man in the suit, "this is Aleks. The one over there is Fred. They are holding me hostage for thirty-seven thousand dollars. Give it to them."

"Signora Bongiorno is, uh, a little harsh, Sir," said Aleks in heavily accented English. "Let us say instead, that we are business associates, and that the signora has a slight, a very slight, cash flow problem. That is what you say, yes? Cash flow?"

"Yes," said Bryce. He sat in an upholstered chair facing a window, which gave him a view of a green park in heavy smog. He looked from Aleks to Brenda to Fred. He kept going in English.

"Is someone going to tell me what this is about?"

The three looked at each other.

"Actually, Bryce, this is not a good idea," said Brenda. "Our business is full of unscrupulous competitors who would stop at nothing to undermine our progress."

"Well, I'm not one of them. Your progress in what, exactly?"

Brenda glowered. "None of your business! You bring the money, that's all you need to do. Then you shut up."

"I don't think so. Before you get the money, I need to know that I'm not breaking the law or doing anything, any little tiny thing, which might have legal implications. Anything that would imply, for instance, a long-term reservation for me in some Albanian dungeon."

Bryce looked at Brenda, but listened to Aleks and Fred as they moved over to the window and spoke in Albanian. Brenda shrugged and poured herself the last of the coffee.

"You're just being silly, Bryce. Besides, they could just take the money from you."

Aleks and Fred continued to discuss the situation.

Bryce's new phone rang, and he answered it. "Bryce here." Then, a minute later, "Yes, just as you said. Your guy ready? Okay!"

He looked toward the two men. "Aleks," he said cheerfully, "this call seems to be for you."

Very suspiciously, Aleks took the phone, stared into it, and slowly brought it to his ear.

"Yes?" he said in English, and then listened.

"Oh, yes, sir," he answered, and then listened for several minutes, then switched to Albanian and launched into a long explanation, glancing from time to time at Brenda. And then finally, still in Albanian, a quiet, "Yes, sir, certainly. Of course. Thank you, sir." and he handed the phone back to Bryce.

"Thanks so much," Bryce said into the phone , "How was it on your end? . . . Oh? . . . That's just what Stevie predicted. Is Stevie still there? . . . Well, please thank him for me. He was very generous to help Brenda. Tell him I think he's a prince."

Aleks spoke rapidly with Fred, still in Albanian, and they both eyed Bryce cautiously. Brenda was speechless with rage.

Bryce undid his belt, took it to the coffee table, carefully opened it, and removed the contents; he then opened his wallet, fished in his jacket pockets, and took off his shoes, retrieving in all thirty-seven thousand of Uncle Mel's dollars.

"I believe this settles everything between you and Ms. – Signora – Bongiorno, yes?"

"Yes, yes," said Aleks. "And please believe me, really we knew nothing of any, uh, family connections."

He offered a hand, and Bryce shook it. Aleks turned to Brenda, bowed, and said, "Signora Bongiorno, I hope you are satisfied with this happy outcome."

"Just get out," growled Brenda.

"Good-bye, then," said Aleks.

Fred the wrestler, who had not spoken a word so far, bowed to Brenda, bowed to Bryce, and carefully said "Gud. Bah-yee."

Brenda eyed Bryce bitterly. "You festering piece of shit! You asshole!"

"You're welcome."

"This is not funny. You called Stevie. I can't believe you called Stevie. I'll never be able to work in Albania again."

"Damn straight you're not going to work in Albania again, or any place else. How many times have you pulled this trick?"

"This is my first time, and it's absolutely brilliant, and I'll make a fortune."

"No more you won't. Stevie says that this is your last time, and that you'll have to give it all back."

"Stevie can go jump off the Atlantic City pier – in cement boots."

"Brenda, honest to God, if you try this again you're going to be the one facing Stevie, and you should be afraid!"

"Hah! Me? Afraid of Stevie?"

But she was, he could see, and as she took in the bad news, she wilted. He had never known her to be so compliant. She took her crutches and hobbled over to the bed. "Help me pack, why don't you?" she said. He got her things together, accompanied her to the front desk, and watched as she checked out. He hailed a cab, and they were off to the airport.

After a substantial wait they boarded a plane in first class, where, once Brenda was settled, the flight attendant offered to put her crutches in a locker.

"No!" said Brenda. "They're staying right here with me. What if I need to go to the toilet?" The toilets were five steps from her seat.

The plane rose in the air and headed east toward Istanbul. The flight attendant offered drinks. Brenda took Scotch; Bryce had a glass of wine. Brenda downed her drink and ordered another. "They were speaking Albanian," she said. "You understood them."

"I told you last time. *One Hundred Phrases for Doing Business in Albania.* I got another copy and memorized them all over again."

"I don't believe you." She looked at him distrustfully. "I don't believe one word of it."

In Istanbul they took a plane to Rome, from there flew to New York, and then to Seattle. As the plane descended into Sea-Tac through dark clouds, Bryce said to Brenda, "I have something to tell you. You need to listen to me."

Brenda closed her eyes. "Fuck off."

"You've been smuggling protected historical objects out of Greece through Albania. I know, and more importantly, Stevie knows. Necklaces and bracelets from the time of Alexander the Great can't be legally taken out of Greece. Stevie can't help you if you get caught."

"Fuck off."

"Brenda!"

"I heard you. Get me another drink."

"It's too late. We're arriving in Seattle. Brenda, I'm serious. Getting caught by police will be easy compared to what will happen to you if you get caught messing around like this by Stevie. You were married to him – who do you think he is?"

"I said fuck off."

They stood up to get off the plane, Brenda hobbling on her crutches. They got a ride on the handicapped cart to baggage claim, where they picked up Brenda's luggage. Uncle Mel was waiting on the curb next to his tubby old Lincoln.

"Brenda! Bryce! Here!"

Mel embraced his sullen daughter and put her huge suitcases in the trunk and then reached for Bryce's backpack.

"No, thanks. I'll keep it. Let me help Brenda into the car." Bryce courteously opened the door and held Brenda's crutches as she moved into the passenger seat. Once she was settled, Bryce closed the door, keeping the crutches.

"Hey! Hey! Give me the crutches!" she cried.

"Bye-bye," he said. "Uncle Mel, my car is here at the airport. I'll see you later." Mel looked surprised, then shrugged and pulled the car out into the stream of traffic, Brenda screaming out the window.

Bryce walked back into the airport, looked around and found a dark, curly-haired man wearing a generic gray uniform with "Bongiorno" embroidered on the chest pocket. Bryce approached him and introduced himself. "I found these crutches lying in the street," Bryce said to him. I thought somebody should take a look at them. Can't be too careful, you know," he said, looking thoughtfully at the crutches, "They seem heavier than you would think for aluminum." "Thank you," the uniformed man replied. Mr. Bongiorno sends his congratulations." And Bryce walked out the door and caught the shuttle to long-term parking, where he had left his car.

Letter from Stefano Bongiorno to Bryce Hanford:

Dear Bryce,

Thank you for handling everything efficiently and discreetly. My Greek contacts have found a museum in Athens that has accepted the artifacts as a gift, and won't investigate their provenance. I am sending an associate to explain to Brenda that her plans are not, in the long run, in her best interest. I'm hoping that you have rescued her for the last time. I owe you.

Stevie

CHAPTER NINE

Back safely on Eliza Island, Bryce felt uneasy. Sooner or later Brenda would want to know how he had known about her smuggling and how he knew that the jewelry was in the crutches. So what? he asked himself. What's the problem? So she figured out that I understood Aleks and Fred speaking in Albanian and she's curious. Why do I care? It wasn't as if he had done anything illegal. But he was glad he hadn't told her about the Bookstore of Other Languages. It was too strange. On the other hand, he had told Stevie about the bookstore, and knowing that Stevie knew was disquieting.

Bryce had come home to find packages and cards piled up for him – his fortieth birthday had come and gone while he was in Albania. The next time they met, the Friday Study Group bought him drinks and toasted him. Justin and Kendra gave him a birthday card and a gift card to the Crab Pot. He got a birthday e-mail from Marina telling him that she was back in France, which was a surprise. He heard nothing from Astrid. Time went by, but the worry and hurt of how she had slipped away, back across a continent and an ocean, was never far away. He had the feeling of running endlessly while staying in the same place.

The town was the same, the people were the same. The only change was the appearance of a mysterious man who had rented an apartment in the block near Bryce's shop. Nobody seemed to know him, and the general speculation was that even though he looked like an off-duty cop, with his gym-trained body, blond crewcut, and trim mustache, he was probably an aspiring writer. He drank coffee and typed into his laptop at Mr. D's during the day and drank beer and typed into his laptop at the Crab Pot in the evening. The Study Group hadn't managed to learn who he was, but then again, they didn't much care, although Ginnie thought at first he was attractive, but then changed her mind.

The most exciting thing going on, as far as Bryce knew, was that Kendra and Bryce were planning their wedding. Like so many other brides and grooms, they found that even "simple" weddings had their complications. Fortunately both sets of parents lived near Seattle. They wound up planning to marry at Kendra's family's long-time church; the pastor had baptized Kendra twenty-three years earlier.

On a Saturday in February Bryce drove himself onto the first ferry of the day. There were only two other cars - the one that Justin and Kendra shared, and a silver Hyundai occupied by the Aspiring Writer, who took his laptop with him to the ferry's galley and typed away as usual. Bryce met Justin and Kendra in the galley and not only bought them coffee, but surprised them with a box of smoked salmon, bagels, and cream cheese, a hearty breakfast for the strenuous day ahead.

At the church Kendra left them to go put on her wedding dress. Bryce, the best man, wore his one and only suit; Justin's father, Mike, met him with a rented suit, and Justin took it into the men's room. A few dozen friends were gathered in the small Lutheran church, which had been decorated with dozens of pots of yellow narcissus and white tulips.

Kendra's mother took her seat in the pew, tucking away her to-do list into her handbag. Justin's parents sat across the aisle from her, his mother in a beige lace dress, his father sporting a lurid purple floral vest under his dark gray suitcoat. Justin and Bryce took their places, the pastor stood in front of the altar, and the organist began to play a gentle melody that Bryce later learned was the national hymn of Norway. Kendra appeared on her father's arm, dressed in the full traditional Norwegian bridal costume that her mother had worn thirty years earlier, followed by her sister, Allison, the maid of honor, also in Norwegian dress. In spite of his suspicion that few Norwegian brides wore this kind of finery anymore, Bryce found himself touched by the appeal to tradition.

After a simple reception, the bride and groom and their families went out for dinner after the service to Kendra's parents' favorite Chinese restaurant. Bryce found himself seated at dinner next to Allison, who had never mastered using chopsticks. He showed her the trick of tapping their ends together so that they were even, and she laughed as she succeeded in lifting a mouthful of food with them. She was a veterinarian and spent the rest of the meal urging him to get a dog. So many available at the animal shelters, and pound puppies were so much healthier than overbred purebreds! Bryce nodded, and even asked questions, thinking that this was as good a way to make the time pass as any other.

Justin and Kendra changed clothes, and Justin's parents drove them to the airport. Bryce drove off, too, arriving in plenty of time to make a late ferry. The silver Hyundai was six cars behind him.

With Justin and Kendra gone on their honeymoon, Bryce had to close the store for a long weekend while he drove to Portland for Roger's birthday. He wondered what Linda was planning to do to top Roger's seventieth birthday, but then decided that she was probably wise enough not to try. He had set himself the goal that day of driving carefully, enjoying the mild weather and the signs of spring, and not using the journey to examine his life. He was only partly successful; instead of examining his own life, he wondered how Justin and Kendra were doing. He thought about their parents: Kendra's mother and her to-do list, Justin's father and his gaudy vest, and the baggage that each person brings to a marriage. Preoccupied as he was, he failed to notice the silver Hyundai that had followed him at a discreet distance all the way to Southeast Portland.

It was pleasant to be greeted affectionately by Roger and Linda, who were so genuinely happy to see him. Sally kissed him, Kenny shook hands, and Connor and Cole stopped racing around the house just long enough to wave to him. Uncle Mel shook hands and shook his head at the same time.

"I don't know, Bryce. I just don't know about your Cousin Brenda."

"What's up, Uncle Mel?" Bryce asked, cursing himself silently for asking.

"I don't just don't know. She's in Portland one day, Seattle the next, she's all over."

"What's she doing in Seattle?"

"You haven't heard from her? I hoped you might have."

"Nothing. But you know, she's pretty mad at me."

Mel shook his head. "I just don't know."

Connor and Cole continued to race around the house while the grown-ups drank coffee and caught up with one another. By the time the party moved into the kitchen to begin work on dinner, the boys had settled into computer games. The conversations continued as garlic and eggplant slices were put into the oven, along with a chicken. A salad was made, the table was set, Kenny opened the first bottle of wine, and all took their seats.

After dinner, Roger opened and admired his presents, being especially charmed by a selection of fake mustaches (from Connor) and tiny dry socks that expanded in water, revealing a pattern of roadrunners (from Cole). The evening wound down, and Kenny and Sally left, each with a boy in hand. Uncle Mel took his leave, continuing to shake his head.

That night Bryce couldn't sleep. He looked around and found his father's old bathrobe hanging companionably next to his mother's old bathrobe in the guest room closet. He pulled it on and went downstairs, surprised to see the kitchen light on. He walked in as Roger was stirring chocolate into warm milk.

"Here – you want this one?" Roger asked. "I'll just make myself another." He handed the warm cup to Bryce, poured milk into another cup and put it in the microwave.

"I have insomnia," said his father. "What's your excuse?"

"I don't have insomnia," said Bryce. "I just can't sleep."

"Something you want to tell your wise old father about?"

Bryce looked at his father. Roger shrugged.

"Okay, not so wise, but I can listen."

"Dad, it's a long story, and the thing is, it's just not believable."

"Bryce, I have known you for forty years. There are things that you haven't told me – and on the whole, I'm convinced that most of those are things I never wanted to know – but I bet you haven't lied to me for at least thirty-five years. What's going on?"

To his great surprise, Bryce unbuttoned. Everything that he had been afraid or unable to tell anyone got told in that long conversation in the night. Bryce told his father about his health scare, his discovery of the Bookstore of Other Languages, his first trip to Albania, about his affair with Marina, his three weeks in Paris and meeting Astrid, about Marina's cancer and Astrid's visit, and finally, about the second trip to Albania and his collaboration with Stevie, and about his confusion and pain about Astrid. Besides saying "You never told us about that!" about the health scare and "Oh, God, Brenda!" Roger listened silently.

"So?" asked Bryce.

"So what?"

"So what should I do?"

"You know, my first response is to say something stupid and jokey, but I don't have the heart to. Bryce, I don't know, I don't know." Roger shook his head, in a rare moment of re-sembling Mel.

"I don't either. I don't even know if there's anything to do. I ask myself if all this happened to somebody else, somebody different from me, to Kenny or one of my friends? What would they do? I can't begin to imagine."

"This would never happen to Kenny."

"Right."

"Thank you for telling me. If I think of anything to tell you, I'll call."

"It's a huge relief for me to tell somebody about it. I'm glad it was you."

They went back to bed, each turning on a light and opening a book. Bryce began a history of the Northwest Coast Native Americans; Roger read *The New Annotated Sherlock Holmes*, his birthday gift from Bryce.

The next day Bryce drove home, the silver Hyundai six cars behind him.

After two weeks of working overtime, Bryce was happy to welcome Justin and Kendra back from their honeymoon. Justin was relaxed and tanned from being in Hawaii; his cheeks were a little redder, and a little rounder, too. Kendra had more freckles, and looked tense. Bryce refrained from asking questions and things went on more or less as they had before.

The next week, Kendra shocked them and herself by snapping at a customer. Poor Mrs. Schroeder, owner of the late

Fritzi, had gotten a new puppy and came in for a dog activity monitor. Kendra appeared to be her usual self, but when Mrs. Schroeder vacillated between the blue and the green versions, Kendra got impatient, and when Mrs. Schroeder said that she couldn't be sure, but she thought that perhaps Schatzi would prefer a flamingo color, Kendra told her to go see how many doggy activity monitors she could buy over at the paint store. Kendra then glared helplessly at Mrs. Schroeder, burst into tears, and ran into the office. Justin and Bryce looked at one another. Justin followed Kendra into the office and Bryce soothed Mrs. Schroeder.

At the end of the day, Bryce suggested a round of beers at the Crab Pot, and they accepted gratefully.

"So," he said, looking at them across the booth, "what's going on?"

They looked at one another.

"What?" asked Bryce.

Kendra waved her arms in the air. "It's our parents. They're driving me crazy. My parents decided after the wedding that Justin's parents should've paid for part of the wedding – it's really my mom. She got the bills and decided that Justin's parents should have to pay for some of them, but of course she had never asked them before the wedding. So, being my mom, she didn't call them up or talk it over, she just sent them the bill from the florist for all the flowers."

Justin continued. "So, then my father got all offended and angry and he called Kendra's mom up and yelled at her."

"And then," said Kendra, "my mom started making comments about the purple vest he wore to the wedding."

Bryce winced. "Not good."

"No," Kendra said.

Justin forged ahead. "We're hoping that Kendra's father and my mother can straighten everything out, but what we think is that we're married now and we are a new family and we don't have to get involved." He looked defiantly at Kendra.

"Except," said Kendra mournfully, "it's the bills from our wedding."

Bryce saw vistas of opportunities opening for their education in marital communication.

E-mail from Roger to Bryce:

Hi, Bryce – I've been thinking about your situation and I still don't have any wise advice for you. I do have some foolish advice, though. I think you should go to Paris.

Dad

Bryce booked a ticket to Paris. He called The Bookstore of Other Languages and made an appointment.

E-mail from Bryce to Astrid:

Dear Astrid,

I'm coming to Paris on a whim (never thought I'd see myself write that!). Is there any chance your apartment is free? If not, can you recommend anything similar or nearby?

I'll arrive in Paris on March 28 and will stay for two weeks. I'm hoping to see you, but it's very much up to you.

Bryce

In late March, Bryce drove to Seattle and parked outside the Bookstore of Other Languages. He walked in the door, and saw Dr. Milton was standing in his office, one arm propped against the doorway, blocking Cilla, who was standing in the office.

Cilla saw Bryce, and said loudly, "Oh, hello, Mr. Hanford!"

Milton dropped his arm and shrugged as Cilla hurried to greet Bryce. They made their way to the treatment room, and all went as usual. As Bryce was leaving he noticed a silver Hyundai parked in the next block. True, there were many silver cars on the road, but even so, it seemed familiar. He got into his car, and pulled out from the curb. He began to wonder about the Hyundai and feeling a little foolish, looked to see if it was following him, but it wasn't. He got to long-term parking at the airport and drove to the far end of the lot, watching for the Hyundai, but nobody else was checking in or parking their car. It was nothing.

REPORT: TMS

HANFORD, BRYCE, CLIENT #0022

LANGUAGE, LEVEL OF PROFICIENCY, DURATION, PRICE:

FRENCH, TOURIST, TWO WEEKS: $600

TECHNICIAN: CILLA M.

REASON FOR CONTACT AND PROGNOSIS FOR FUTURE EN-GAGEMENT:

This is Mr. Hanford's fifth session – one of our most successful cases. This is his third purchase of French. Dr. Milton, should we encourage him to consider a purchase of lifetime fluency?

E-mail from Northwest Security Services to Ms. Brenda Bongiorno:

We are pleased to be able to report to you that we have traced Mr. Hanford to the source of his language fluency, a storefront on Elliott Alley in Seattle called The Bookstore of Other Languages, owned by Dr. Daniel Milton. Milton uses transcranial magnetic stimulation to implant language fluency. He is said, by an employee, to be Dutch, but we find no record of a Daniel Milton in the Netherlands. We have found no criminal record in this country, but he may have been involved in a scam in Arizona purporting to reverse Alzheimer's disease through the use of TMS.

We are glad to have brought this investigation to a successful conclusion. Please see the attached photos and invoice.

Very truly yours,

Eric Truman

Northwest Security Services, Inc.

Dr. Daniel Milton was staring at his computer monitor. He stared, but could not change the numbers he saw on his spreadsheet. He continued to stare without results. The bell on the door rang, and he turned to see a voluptuous woman in high heels, gold jewelry, and a leopard skin coat moving through the bookstore and toward his office. She stopped in his doorway and smiled.

"Are you the owner?" she asked.

He took a long look at her.

"I am if you want me to be," he said.

REPORT: INITIAL MAPPING AND TMS

BONGIORNO, BRENDA, CLIENT #0064

INITIAL SCAN: $450

LANGUAGE, LEVEL OF PROFICIENCY, DURATION, PRICE:

FRENCH, TOURIST, ONE WEEK: $300

TECHNICIAN: DR. DANIEL MILTON

REASON FOR CONTACT AND PROGNOSIS FOR FUTURE EN-
GAGEMENT:

Ms. Bongiorno is a wealthy widow interested in world travel. There is every reason to believe that she will become a regular client.

E-mail from Astrid to Bryce:

The apartment is all yours. We're all looking forward to your visit – did you know that Marina came back? She got homesick! Imagine! She's in Brittany with her parents now, but plans to come to Paris to see you. School is back in session and I'm working, so won't have much time to spend with you. Mama wants to meet you, though, so she would like to invite you to dinner while you're here.

As always,

Astrid

Bryce arrived in an exceptionally cold Paris on a Thursday. He picked up the key at the music shop, and he made his way up three flights of stairs to the tiny apartment where he found a note on the table. "Dear Bryce – Welcome! Please join us for dinner tomorrow evening. We're on the second floor of the apartment building just to the left of the Breton Restaurant where we had dinner, on rue de Montparnasse. 7:30. Astrid."

He unpacked and went out to buy groceries, but wound up having dinner alone at that same Breton restaurant, thinking of Astrid (and her mother) being so near. He treated himself to a dinner of lobster and rice and walked back in the dark frosty night. She had made the bed for him, but the apartment was chilly – he had forgotten to turn the heat on before he went out. He turned on the reading lamp, undressed, slid in between cold sheets, and opened a book.

Springtime in Paris, ha! Bryce thought the next morning, looking out the window at gray skies and sleet. It wasn't a day for idle wandering, and he decided to do something radically different from what he had done in his earlier visit – he went shopping. He found the renowned department store on the right bank to be impressive, but then the height of his department store experience until now was the Nordstrom flagship store in Seattle. He strolled through the jewelry and handbags and unbelievable ladies' shoes and finally found the menswear department, where he bought a tie to wear to dinner with Astrid and her mother. He was wondering what a wealthy New Yorker accustomed to Manhattan's luxury department stores would say about this famous emporium, when he thought he heard a familiar voice lifted in fluently vulgar abuse toward a clerk in the handbag department. The voice was remarkably like Brenda's. Knowing that Brenda had no talent for language, and that it was quite impossible that it was Brenda's voice, but wanting to be gone nonetheless, he carefully retreated to the escalator. He window-shopped his way back to his neighborhood, paying special attention to men's eyeglass frames, feeling that he would soon be in the market for a pair.

He stopped for a coffee and pastry, thinking of his afternoon with Astrid the year before. He stopped by a bookstore
and browsed, finding a book on Haussmann and the long dem-
olition and rebuilding of the city of Paris. He walked the rest
of the way paying special attention to the architecture around
him.

At home, he made himself a sandwich and poured a glass of
water. He opened his new book, read a few pages, and heard a
knock on his door. Expecting, or at least hoping, to find Astrid
at the threshold, he was astonished to see Brenda instead. She
waved him aside and strode into the apartment.

"So! Here's where you're hiding!"

"Brenda, what in God's name are you doing here? I don't
mean Paris, I mean in my apartment."

"I want to have a talk with you." She looked around and sat
in the one comfortable chair and peevishly adjusted the cush-
ions. "Get me a drink."

"Brenda, tell me what you're doing here or so help me God
I will pick up your crippled body and toss it out the window
like they used to do with garbage."

"You mean sewage, but you're too prissy to say so."

"Go ahead, wheedle me for that drink."

"What do you mean crippled? I'm not crippled!"

"Oh, I know you're not. I should have said, your faux-
crippled body."

"You stole my crutches!"

"I returned your stolen loot."

"You called Stevie! I can't believe you called Stevie!"

"Brenda! What do I have to do to get you to leave?"

"Well, now, that's better. First of all, get me a drink."

Bryce took down two glasses and poured red wine into each of them. Brenda snorted, but accepted her glass.

She took a sip and made a face. "Cheap."

"Brenda, what the fuck are you doing here?"

She drank the rest of her wine. "Bryce. Tell me about the Bookstore of Other Languages."

"Jesus, Mary, and Joseph," he implored, drank the rest of his wine, got up, got the bottle, and refilled their glasses. "If you know about the Bookstore then there's not much else I can tell you. You've been there? Oh! Of course you've been there! That was you I heard cursing at the clerk at the department store! You have been to the Bookstore! There's no way you could have learned that much French on your own."

Brenda stared at him.

"How are you involved with them?

"What do you mean, involved with them? I've used their process to be able to speak French, and twice, to my great sorrow, to be able to speak Albanian."

"Who are they? Who's backing them? They're sitting on a gold mine and there they are hidden away in a shithole block of Seattle. What's going on?"

"I don't know. I have not one single idea, Brenda. You're asking the wrong person."

"How did you find them?"

"Brenda, I'm telling you, I know nothing about them. I found them by accident, I used them because it was the best thing I could think of when I was going to fucking Albania, and it works. There – you know everything I know.

She glared at him. "I'm leaving. Don't tell anybody I was here."

"Who would I tell?"

"Don't tell Stevie!"

"Why would I tell Stevie? WHAT is going on?"

"Good-bye!" She stood up, drained her glass, and she was out the door.

He watched her from the window as she stormed down the sidewalk, dodging icy puddles.

On Saturday Bryce shopped for a bottle of wine but then thought perhaps he ought to bring flowers. If the Bookstore were truly great, he thought, he would know these things. He was wearing his new tie and the sport jacket he had packed, hoping he might be able to spend time somehow with Astrid. Armed with his bottle of petit sirah (somebody, he forgot who, had said it was his favorite wine) and a bunch of daffodils (trucked or flown in for God knew where), he walked to Astrid's apartment and rang their bell. The door clicked, he climbed to the second floor, and there was Astrid, standing in the doorway. Dark hair, blue eyes, straight nose, high cheek-bones, dark, arched eyebrows, and all that said nothing compared to how he felt when she was looking at him, in her kindly, but unsparing inspection that encouraged him to in-spect himself, but also to inspect himself kindly.

Mme. Ollivier shared Astrid's coloring, but in a rounder, softer package. Long black lashes batted over huge, deep-set blue eyes. She had Astrid's smile but Marina's temperament.

Her good-humored teasing and flirtatiousness sparkled on the surface rather than rippling underneath.

"At last!" she said. "Ah, but we are friends already, no?" she said, gently laying a hand on each shoulder, pulling him over and kissing him on each cheek. She reeked of cigarettes.

"Mme. Ollivier, it's a great pleasure to meet you."

"Astrid told me that you spoke French so well! How did you get such a good accent?"

Bryce shrugged off the question and presented her with the wine and flowers.

"I love Americans!" she said. "But we are not so formal as you think. Call me Thérèse, my dear."

She poured him a glass of wine.

Thérèse asked about Eliza Island, curious about who Eliza might have been.

"The true story is that it was named after a Spanish explorer, Francisco de Eliza. The romantic story is that it was named by an English explorer after his fiancée, who died before he returned to England. The sad story is that the romantic story isn't true, but since most people don't care, it doesn't matter."

"Oh, you are cynical!"

The conversation stretched out over the evening. Bryce asked about Haussmann's renovation of the city, and Astrid had much to say about it. Thérèse countered her daughter's dryer account of Parisian neighborhoods with anecdotes and gossip about them. Dinner was pork with mustard sauce, bread, salad, and wine. Over cheese and walnuts, and a hot, sweet, strong drink that he did not recognize, Bryce asked about the family.

"Astrid told me briefly about how she is Marina's age and still her aunt, but I have to confess I didn't understand. Can you explain these mysteries to me, Thérèse?"

"It isn't so very hard, my dear. My late husband, Hervé, was born in 1930. His family ran a restaurant in Rennes. As a young man he married Annette. Their son, Yves, married Juliette, and their daughter is Marina. Annette died, though, in 1953, when Yves was a baby. Hervé's mother and sisters took care of Yves, and Hervé did nothing but work, and opened up two more restaurants, including the one in Paris. When Yves was grown up, Hervé realized that he was rich and in his fifties and single. He married me and we had Astrid. See? Simple?"

"I thought that the man running the Paris restaurant was Hervé."

"Hervé's sister's son, Astrid and Marina's cousin, named after his uncle."

"It makes my head spin."

"That's the chouchen that you've been drinking. It's a traditional liquor of Brittany."

All during the evening since dinner, Astrid had been very quiet. As Bryce got ready to leave, Astrid put on her coat and hat and gloves. "I'll walk you home," she said.

It was very dark outside and the sidewalks were icy. "Be careful," Astrid said, and took his arm.

He whirled around to face her. "Astrid!"

"What? What is it?"

"Sorry I yelled." He took a deep breath. "Astrid, will you marry me?"

Astrid looked at him in distress, said nothing for a while, and started walking again. "Marina told me that she told you my story."

"I'm so sorry that you had to live through that horrible experience!"

She stopped walking and smiled at him under lifted eyebrows.

"No! No! That's not what I mean! No, I'm very very glad you lived through it! I'm just sorry . . . oh, I'm tangled up!"

They walked a block and crossed a street.

Astrid stopped and looked at him. "Do you understand that the right side of my chest looks like a battlefield?"

"Is it like Marina's??

"Her battlefield is my battlefield."

"I've already seen it. I don't care."

She took his arm and walked with him down the sidewalk toward his apartment. He stopped again and turned her to face him.

"Astrid. Will you marry me?"

"Bryce, what would happen to us? How would we live together?"

"You're thinking about it!"

They stopped in front of the apartment building. She kissed him on the cheek. He looked in her eyes and found nothing.

"I'm dying here," he said. "What? What?"

"I'll be at the apartment tomorrow before noon. We'll talk then."

E-mail from Brenda Bongiorno to Stefano Bongiorno:

Listen to me, Stevie, you have to listen to me! I've come across something worth a fortune and it's beyond me. I'm going to tell you about it and if you make any money I want a cut.

You need to look into this place in Seattle, The Bookstore of Other Languages. They have some high-tech way of putting language into your head. It's true. I saw it at work both times when Bryce was in Albania. The first time he was speaking Albanian with the people at the hospital where I was and in the stores and with the travel people. I heard him! When he came to pay those disgusting thugs in Tirana, he understood them when they were talking to one another. It's the only way he could have known about the jewelry being in my crutches. You're both such bastards!

So then I went to Seattle to see for myself. I chatted up the owner, Dr. Daniel Milton, and I bought a week of tourist French for $300. They do it with some kind of medical procedure called TMS. Stevie, it worked! It fucking worked! I went to Paris and I just talked and understood other people.

There's something weird going on with this outfit. Why aren't they famous? Why are they hidden away in a sleazy part of Seattle? Why don't they have hundreds of people from businesses wanting to expand their market? Imagine going in there and coming out with Mandarin! The whole thing is so damn furtive. I wish you'd let me help – I've got Milton eating out of my hand. I know I could convince him to sell to you for nothing. But however you do it, you owe me a cut!

Brenda

Stefano Bongiorno to Benjamin Goh, M.D., PhD., M.B.A.:
Dear Ben,

Since our collaboration on the medical and pharmaceutical branch of Bongiorno Enterprises has been such a success, I wonder if you'd be interested in expanding into a related field. There's a poorly-run business in Seattle, The Bookstore of Other Languages, that claims to provide language fluency through transcranial magnetic stimulation. Oddly enough, I've heard about it from two sources – one that I trust and one that I don't. Will you look into it? If you conclude that it has potential, we can discuss how best to acquire and develop it.

Best,

Stevie

On Sunday, Astrid appeared at Bryce's door, walked into his arms and fell with him into his bed, where they remained, except for brief pauses for food, for the rest of the day.

As darkness fell, Astrid wrapped a blanket around herself and went to turn the heat up, sat on the bed and faced Bryce. "What's going to happen to us?"

"We're going to get married. We're going to live happily ever after."

"In what country? On what money? What happens to Mama? Do I move to Eliza Island? Do you move to Paris? What?"

"I'll work on it."

Astrid wailed and buried her face in his chest. "I should never have let this happen!"

"Astrid! Do you mean that?"

"No!"

He sighed and held her closer.

"Yes!"

He tightened his grasp on her and rocked her back and forth.

"Don't do this. What do you think? That it's all over when it's just started?"

"Oh, I give up. Bryce!"

"No! Don't give up!"

"I don't mean that kind of giving up. I mean the other giving up."

"Yes? What?"

"Oh, this is so scary! Oh, Bryce – I love you."

"Good. I love you, too."

The numbers on Dr. Milton's spreadsheet had not improved on the day that a balding, middle-aged Chinese gentlemen entered the Bookstore of Other Languages. Looking up from his computer, Milton saw the visitor happily taking pictures with his phone.

"Excuse me!" Milton said loudly.

"Hello!" said the newcomer, smiling broadly. "I'm so pleased to have found you! I think you can help me."

Milton suppressed a desire to grab the man's phone and stomp on it.

"May I ask why you were taking pictures?"

"Oh, it's a long story. Let me start at the beginning. My name is Benjamin Goh. My family in Hong Kong wants to acquire paintings – Dutch genre paintings from the seventeenth century. They'd prefer ter Borch, but they'd be willing to widen the search if necessary."

Milton shifted his weight from one foot to the other. "I don't think I can help you with that," he said impatiently.

"Well, you can in a way," Goh said. "I'm going to the Netherlands to talk with auction houses and collectors, and it would really help if I spoke Dutch. I believe you can help me with that. Yes?"

"Oh, well, yes. That's what we do here. And the reason you were taking photos?"

"For my family back in Hong Kong! They want me to keep them informed about my progress. They can be . . ." Mr. Goh shrugged, "Oh, you know . . . they want all the information they can get. You know families. Or maybe you don't know Chinese families."

"No. No, I don't."

"You are the owner of this business?"

"Yes, Dr. Daniel Milton."

"It's a pleasure to meet you, Dr. Milton!" said Goh, grabbing Milton's hand and shaking it vigorously. "May I ask, well, you know, the family is curious, where you studied and what your doctorate is in?"

Milton's eyes roamed over the bookshelves, then came back to Goh.

"I studied neuropsychology and linguistics in Europe. Your family wouldn't have heard of these programs. They are small, elite institutions whose research is funded by select benefactors."

"Oh, how impressive! Well, then, I'd like to learn Dutch. How does that work?"

Milton explained the levels of fluency and the charges for each.

"As it happens, Mr. Goh, our treatment room is free now. Let's go next door."

As they walked out onto the sidewalk and into the clinic, Milton turned to Goh.

"Mr. Goh, how did you happen to hear about our business?"

"Oh, my good friend Bryce Hanford told me about it."

"Mr. Hanford has used our services several times."

"Yes, he recommends you highly."

REPORT: INITIAL MAPPING AND TMS

GOH, BENJAMIN, CLIENT #0076

INITIAL SCAN: $450

LANGUAGE, LEVEL OF PROFICIENCY, DURATION, PRICE: DUTCH, NATIVE SPEAKER, ONE WEEK: $750

TECHNICIAN: DR. DANIEL MILTON

REASON FOR CONTACT AND PROGNOSIS FOR FUTURE ENGAGEMENT:

Mr. Goh is traveling to the Netherlands to negotiate the purchase of Dutch paintings from his family in Hong Kong. I want the staff to know that I don't trust him. I actually caught him taking pictures of the store! From now on don't allow anyone to take pictures. And if Goh shows up again I want to know about it.

E-mail from Astrid to Marina:

Yes, I'm in love, yes he loves me, yes we did it. Now I'm totally confused, don't see how this is ever going to work out, and I think I'm going to wind up with a broken and smashed heart because

I've lost this good man. If it's anything to you, Mama adores him. I
hope you're satisfied.

    Astrid

    p.s. If you touch him again I'll murder you.

The day before Bryce was to go home, Marina came to Paris
for a visit. She met Bryce and Astrid in a café, whirling in
through the revolving door, brushing rain off her newly chin-
length hair, and radiant with happiness for them. She embraced and kissed them both.

She ordered a coffee, and joined them at a window table.

"Marina," said Bryce sternly, "you have a great deal to answer for! Sit there and give us an account of yourself."

She continued to beam at them both.

"There's too much to tell. The bottom line is that I'm taking
a vacation from always being on vacation. I've promised myself one entire year of living as a grown-up person in Rennes.
I'll find a job, massage as always, and see what it's like being in
one place for more than a few months."

"Where will you work? Is there a hospital there?" asked
Bryce.

"Bryce, duh. There's a university hospital there. It's a big
city. It's the capital city of Brittany."

"Okay, okay, just making sure. I'm sure Dr. Martini will
miss you. Will miss both of you."

Marina grinned teasingly. "Which one of us are you jealous
of?"

"Both of you! But now that you mention it, Marina, if you should decide to come back to Washington, you have my permission to reel Dr. Martini in. If you like older guys, that is."

"What about you two? Have you figured out what to do?"

Astrid and Bryce looked at one another.

"No," Astrid said, "but I have decided that the answer is there. It's just waiting for us to discover it."

Bryce smiled.

CHAPTER TEN

Bryce promptly went to work ready to begin solving the Bryce-and-Astrid problem. At the end of the next work day, he spoke to Justin and Kendra.

"I need to talk with you both. Can I buy you breakfast tomorrow?"

They exchanged glances. Justin spoke. "Bryce, the last time you bought us breakfast you told us that Marina had breast cancer. What now?"

"It's not that bad. In fact, it's mostly not bad at all, just complicated. My life has become complicated. I'm trying to make it simple, but I don't see how right now."

Kendra flipped her braids back. "You're asking us? What do we know? We're still trying to figure out our mommies and daddies."

"How's that going, by the way?"

"We told my parents that in our opinion they were being unreasonable; we told Justin's parents that in our opinion they didn't owe my parents anything; and we told them all that that was the last time they were going to hear anything from us on the subject."

Bryce smiled. "You guys are great. I tell you what – you have dinner plans?"

They exchanged glances, shrugged, and shook their heads.

"Instead of breakfast tomorrow, how about I order a pizza and go get some beer right now? I could get a fancy pizza – prosciutto and fennel?"

"Who are we to argue?" said Justin. "Why not?"

Provisions at hand, they cleared Bryce's desk and sat in a convivial and conspiratorial huddle, while Bryce told them about Astrid. "Good for you!" said Justin. Kendra shook her head. "Bryce, just in case you haven't noticed, I want to draw your attention to the fact that Astrid is totally gorgeous."

"You know what? I'm slow, but I'm not that slow. I had figured that out some time ago."

They all sipped their beers and looked smug.

"So?" said Justin, smiling into his broad cheeks, "Where are you going to live?"

Bryce made a face. "That's the problem. Astrid lives in Paris with her mother and near other relatives, and has a good job that she likes. I live here, far from a city, but in a beautiful place, a day's drive from my family, and I own a business. We're stuck. If either of you gets any brilliant ideas, let me know."

And on that note, they packed up the trash, moved the desks back, shut up the shop, and went home.

Bryce made the same report to the Friday Study Club that he had made to Justin and Kendra. His story was received with much the same good-will, although with considerably more comment.

"You went on a 'voyage of self-discovery,' and look where it got you," said Ginnie, whose one long silver tress now included a streak of purple.

"I like where it got me, at least so far. We just can't figure out the next steps."

Ashley said, "Let's look at it another way. There are two problems, really. One is the nobody-wants-to-leave-their-family problem. The other is the nobody-wants-to-quit-their-job-or-lose-their-business problem. Yes?"

Hal and Ginnie and Bryce nodded.

"I could move to France," said Bryce.

"Where would you work?" asked Ashley. "Not to mention where would you get Mexican food?"

"Well, I'm not sure about either question. There must be tech jobs there I could do. Maybe Carlos could open a branch of Lo Tengo in Paris."

Ashley brightened. "Ooohh. Yes!"

Ginnie said, "What about families? Yours and hers."

"The airlines are still in business last time I looked. We could visit."

Ginnie's purple tress waved back and forth as she slowly shook her head. "I know that Astrid lives with her mother. What if both she and her mother lived here? Would that work?"

"I don't know," said Bryce. "Just wait till you meet Thérèse." He sighed. "You're forgetting the really big problem. It's
the Bryce-doesn't-speak-French problem. I could imagine sell-
ing the business and moving to France. The problem is the
language. Without the language, how would I ever get a job?
How would I make friends or just get around?"

Hal looked at him. "How did you get around in Paris when
you were there? I know they say that everybody speaks English, but I don't believe it."

Bryce came to a great decision. "My friends, prepare yourselves, order new drinks if you need to. I am going to tell you a
marvelous and unbelievable tale. The only reason I haven't
told you the marvelous part is because of the unbelievable
part."

He had their attention and he told them about The
Bookstore of Other Languages.

"So I could solve everything if I had a hundred thousand
dollars," he said, and looked around at his friends.

"Ye-e-e-e-s?" they said.

"I'd take the money to the Bookstore and buy a lifetime of
native-speaker French. Move to France, get a job, marry Astrid
– not in that order – boom! Problem solved."

"Sell your business?"

"That might do it. I can't imagine who would buy it, but after all, I bought it. Am I hearing an offer?"

Three heads shook.

"But there are brokers for that sort of thing," said Ashley.
"Who knows? Seattle might be full of people who dream about

moving to romantic Eliza Island, if only they could find a computer business for sale."

"What if I sell the business and then Astrid decides to come here?"

Hal, ever logical, pulled a small notebook out of his shirt pocket, opened to a new page, clicked his mechanical pencil, and said, "Can't hurt to write it down."

Bryce was willing, and they went through various solutions to the problem, but when Hal had finished with his cost-benefit analysis of each solution, and they all looked at the results, their faces fell.

At this point, his friends became cranky and restless and decided it was time to go home. Bryce couldn't blame them.

"What if I moved to Eliza Island and Mama came with me?" asked Astrid when they skyped, early in her morning and late in Bryce's night.

"Can Thérèse live where there are no men to flirt with?"

"Aren't there any single men on Eliza Island?" asked Astrid. "She's not going to marry any of them, you know."

"We could move to Seattle. Would that be better?"

"Maybe." Astrid smiled. "There are more men there. Could I teach history and geography in an American high school?"

"There are ritzy private schools, too. Try the Caldwell School and Academy Portia."

"I will. Also, I want to tell you, in case you don't already know, Rennes is the center of France's internet technology. There are all kinds of high-tech businesses there."

"Oh, really? That opens up possibilities. I'll look into jobs there.

"How could you even think of leaving your family?"

"We can't think that way. We just have to keep looking for a solution. It won't be ideal, it'll just be the best we can do and that will have to be enough. I worry about the language problem – my high school French isn't going to be enough and it will take me years to really be fluent."

They stopped talking and looked at one another. Bryce blew out a long breath of air.

"I love you," he said to her image on the monitor.

"I love you," she answered and reached out a finger to touch the screen.

He shook himself. "How's Marina?"

"I don't believe her. She's having coffee with her friends from the lycée; she's having drinks with all the single men!"

"Is it so hard to believe that Marina would be having drinks with single men?"

"Bryce, you don't understand. These are men she went to school with. They were confirmed in the same church. Her parents know their parents."

"Oh. Well, now that you put it that way, I get it. But you know what? She's probably the most exciting thing to hit Rennes since the second Dreyfus trial."

"You've been reading up!"

"I can't put it down. Pride and honor versus telling the truth. It's an eternal situation."

"When you come back, I'll take you to the great Montparnasse cemetery. Dreyfus is buried there."

"I went there and looked for him, but couldn't find him."

"Obviously, you need me."

"Yeah."

Tourists to the city of Leiden, in the Netherlands on the Old Rhine, can visit a number of museums, stroll in the beautiful botanical gardens, explore a windmill, or just admire the tulips. Dr. Benjamin Goh took advantage of none of these attractions but instead made for the ancient university, where he walked heedlessly past the Bibliotheca Thysiana (1655) and the famous observatory (1860). Asking for directions in flawless Dutch, he made his way to the department of neuropsychology.

He found the department office, where a cheerful young woman greeted him. He explained that he was trying to locate a Daniel Milton, who may have been awarded a PhD by the department ten or fifteen years earlier. The young woman, a Miss Cuypers, said that she could easily find him, but to her surprise – although not to Goh's – it proved to be impossible. No one by that name had ever been awarded any degree by her department, or, it turned out by any department in the University.

"It's very odd," she said. "Why were you wanting to find him?"

"A colleague and I have a business opportunity with a Daniel Milton. Before we go ahead, we want to double-check his background. I've already failed to find a record in Amsterdam. If I can't find him here I'll have to go on to Rotterdam."

"I'm so sorry – it looks like you have another trip ahead of you."

Just then a pleasant-looking middle-aged woman came in the room.

"Oh, Professor Heijman," said Miss Cuypers, "this gentleman is looking for a Daniel Milton, who might have been a student here some years ago. Do you remember anyone of that name?"

Professor Heijman shook her head. "No, I'm sorry."

"But you were here then?" asked Dr. Goh.

"Yes, I've been here almost twenty years," she answered.

"I have a recent picture of Daniel Milton. Perhaps you might recognize him?"

Professor Heijman took the photograph he offered.

"No . . . no, I don't think so," she said.

"No, wait." The near-sighted professor took off her glasses, and leaned in toward the photograph.

"Oh, my God!"

"What?" Dr. Goh and Miss Cuypers chorused.

Professor Heijman dropped the photo on the desk with a look of distaste. She turned on Dr. Goh.

"What are you doing with Nicolaas Kruse?"

"I've never heard of Nicolaas Kruse. This man calls himself Daniel Milton.

"You better tell me about this," she said sternly.

She led the way into her office, and sat behind her desk. Goh followed her and sat across from her.

"Just what is your interest in Kruse?" Professor Heijmann asked.

"Daniel Milton owns a business that sells language fluency using some sort of medical procedure. A friend and I were thinking of investing in the business."

"Well, don't!" she responded harshly.

Goh waited. She took a breath.

"Nicolaas Kruse was a graduate student here. He was not unintelligent, but not as intelligent as he thought. He was ambitious and very self-confident and resented any criticism, or even advice. He was working with transcranial magnetic stimulation, and convinced another student to undergo a procedure. During the procedure the student suffered a prolonged seizure and had permanent brain damage. Criminal charges against Kruse were dropped, and before the student's family could sue, Kruse had disappeared."

After a moment of silence, Goh said simply, "How horrible."

"Indeed. Dr. Goh, that student and her family would very much like to know how to find Nicolaas Kruse. He owes them a great deal."

After a moment, Goh answered her. "Professor, first of all, let me tell you that even if the family found him, there is no money to be gotten out of him. His business is failing. Do you think that they want some sort of revenge?"

She sighed. "No. No, of course not. They would be glad to know that he's not endangering anyone else. But you said you were considering investing in his business."

"We are thinking of taking over his business. And I truly don't think he's endangering anyone now," Goh said, and then added quietly, "Except himself."

The weeks of separation were painful for both Bryce and Astrid, and in late April she took advantage of the spring academic holiday to return to Eliza Island. Bryce met her at Sea-Tac airport, overcome once more by how beautiful she was and how changed his life was. At the car, they put her luggage in the car, turned to one another and stood in the parking garage, silently embracing. They smiled at one another, smiled again, got in the car, and started the long journey.

They drove through the city to the north. After some silence, Bryce glanced at Astrid.

"There's something I have to tell you," he said.

She raised her eyebrows. "Should I be afraid?"

"I don't think so, but it's such a far-fetched story."

"Far-fetched?"

"Unbelievable. Preposterous."

"Preposterous. That's a good word!"

"Well, it is preposterous." He hesitated and then continued. "Astrid, I haven't wanted to tell you about how I've been speaking – and not speaking – French. In a way it's no big deal, but it's so preposterous I've been afraid you wouldn't believe me and I then I would feel so ridiculous and so I didn't want to tell you and I've kind of dug myself in a hole. So I'm telling you in the car so I don't have to look at you while I'm telling it." And he glanced over at her.

"Oh, my love! Of course I will believe you! And now I'm torn between wanting to reassure you and being very curious! What can it be?"

And so he told her the story of The Bookstore of Other Languages.

When he finished, she said, "You know it's not all that pre-posterous. I have actually heard of TMS. I know someone who was treated for depression with it. But I have never heard of anyone using it to put a language into somebody's head."

"Well, when I first heard about it," he said, "I thought it was crazy. Or I thought I was crazy. It was only when I had to go rescue Brenda that I decided to try it."

She smiled. "And here we are!"

He reached for her hand. "And here we are."

After a few days of being together, Bryce convinced Astrid to drive with him to Portland to meet his family. They drove down I-5, Bryce continuing to reassure her that everything would be fine and that everyone would love her. She wouldn't believe it and fidgeted most of the way, fearing that they could only see her as an evil woman who would lure Bryce to another continent. They pulled up at the house, and Astrid let out one soft extended moan. Bryce squeezed her hand.

Connor and Cole rushed out of the house to greet them, and then became suddenly shy. Astrid extended a hand and the boys stiffly shook it.

"Do you speak English?" asked Connor.

"Yes, indeed! I've studied English since I was eight years old, and that was a long time ago."

"You don't look very old," said Cole. "Not as old as Uncle Bryce."

"That is a very great relief!" said Astrid. "I feel so much better!"

Cole smirked. Connor shoved him. Bryce sighed, a bit with irritation, more with relief.

They went to the door where Linda greeted them somewhat shyly. Roger put a hand on his wife's shoulder and smiled warmly at Astrid, and Bryce knew that something in her body and breathing had eased. Uncle Mel loomed benevolently behind them. Sally and Kenny appeared with welcoming smiles.

Roger decided to open Astrid's gift – a bottle of champagne – before dinner. Linda asked about Astrid's family and the question opened up a stream of family stories, which Linda then matched with oddities from hers and Roger's families. Kenny contributed a story of twin brothers in his grandfather's family who had married twin sisters, and conversation was easy through the champagne and dinner.

"So what's the plan?" asked Kenny. "Come on, you can tell us. What happens next?"

Bryce shrugged. "We don't know. It's all very confusing. Will I move to France? Will Astrid move here? We just don't know."

Sally looked thoughtful. "How about jobs? Bryce, how good is your French?"

"This is a very very long story," said Bryce, "and I'm only going to give you a very edited version." And so, finally, he told them about The Bookstore of Other Languages.

"That's amazing!" said Sally.

"Yeah!" added Kenny. "But how come they're so small? With a system like that how come they're not putting Rosetta Stone out of business?"

"You know," said Bryce, "I've asked myself that, and I just don't have an answer."

"How did you find them?"

"I stumbled on them just walking around the waterfront. But what got me to try them was Brenda."

Uncle Mel looked up. "How was that?"

"The Bookstore of Other Languages was how I got Brenda out of Albania. Both times! I bought a week of business level Albanian. It worked."

"I didn't know anything about this," said Mel, looking puzzled and thoughtful.

Linda asked, "Can't you just buy a lifetime of French? That would solve a few problems."

"I've asked about it. A lifetime of native-speaker French is a hundred thousand dollars. That's a bundle. Even if I sold my business I couldn't do it, and even if I could I'd have the language and nothing else."

Astrid smiled and her eyes slid over to him.

Bryce glanced at her and blinked. "Except Astrid!"

"But what about your mother, Astrid?" asked Linda. Will she come to visit?"

Astrid looked apologetic. "You know," she explained, "Mama is very very French. On one hand that means that she makes herself beautiful and loves conversation and flirting, but on the other hand it means, at least for her generation, that she has smoked almost all her life. I don't think she could make that long flight without cigarettes."

"Could she get a patch?" asked Roger. "It might work."

Astrid sighed. "You'd have to meet my mother. There is the nicotine, that is one thing, but the cigarette is also a theatrical property, a part of her character's costume. She wouldn't be the same character without it."

"I wonder," said Roger, "what that would be for me. What would I not be me without?"

The family's guesses included Roger's bathrobe, his wedding ring, and the *Sunset Book of Western Gardening*. From there the party moved into the kitchen where everyone took turns washing up and putting things away while they guessed the essential props of the others and the conversation wound down from hilarity to sleepy silliness. Sally and Kenny packed up their boys, shook hands with Astrid, and drove off. Uncle Mel followed soon after.

Linda spoke to Bryce and Astrid. "Now, listen to me, you two. We're not going to be embarrassed or silly. I've put you in the same bed, and if you don't like it then Bryce can sleep on the couch. I'm off to my own bed."

Alone in Bryce's childhood bedroom, they found their way into one another's arms.

"I've lived forty years without you," Bryce said to Astrid. "But you are what I wouldn't be me without."

She leaned against him.

At breakfast the next morning, Roger cleared his throat and looked significantly at Bryce and Astrid.

"I have a pronouncement to make and I intend to make it."

He had their attention.

"I propose that this visit has taken care of your duty to Bryce's family. It seems like a very good idea to me that you go back to Washington, get a license, and get married. I know you haven't figured everything out yet, but this is a step that you have figured out. Why not go ahead with it?"

Linda nodded vigorously.

So they did. They drove back, stopping in Seattle to buy simple gold rings. They went to the San Juan county courthouse in Friday Harbor and got a license, and some days later, with Justin and Kendra as witnesses, and in the presence of Ginnie, Hal, and Ashley, they went back to the courthouse and got married.

Stevie leaned back in his office chair and looked at the ceiling. Knowing him well, Dr. Goh waited patiently.

Stevie sat up. "You know, Ben," he said, "it's so bizarre. If Milton – or Kruse – has got this thing to work, it's a huge opportunity for us. It has incredible potential. If it works. He must be a terrible businessman."

"Oh, it works. It worked for Bryce and it worked for me. From what Professor Heijmann told me, I see him as having brains, but basically lazy. He's ambitious, but impatient; wants it now, but doesn't want to work for it."

"It worked for Brenda, too."

"Brenda told you?"

"She doesn't know I heard about it from Bryce. She wants me to buy the business and then give her a cut."

"She doesn't change."

Stevie made a face. "No. She doesn't." He shook his head. "I don't know. It could be great. I don't think we'd need to pay Milton much. We could just threaten to send his whereabouts to Professor Heijmann. Or we could pay him a salary and keep him on as a consultant."

It was Goh's turn to shake his head. "The missing part is the lifetime fluency. With that it's golden. Without that . . . not worth it."

"We need a guinea pig."

"Yeah."

"You are amazing," said Brenda, looking down at the candle on the restaurant table and gently shaking her freshly cut and colored hair.

"No, you are amazing," said Daniel Milton, looking down admiringly at her low-cut snakeskin-print blouse. "How did Bongiorno ever let you get away?"

"I'll tell you," she said wistfully, almost reluctantly. "Every good idea Stevie ever acted on came from my head. I did everything I could to pretend that he was the smart one, but he is – well, the therapist said he was competitive, and I think he couldn't take being around me, no matter how careful I was not to take credit for anything. And believe me, there was a lot to take credit for. So," and here she became very sad, "I lost it all."

Milton beckoned to a waiter and ordered two more glasses of wine. He reached over the table for Brenda's hand.

"Brenda. Don't give up. You're beautiful and brilliant. There are opportunities ahead of you." He slowly rubbed his thumb over her knuckles. "Even better opportunities for the two of us working together."

She looked up into his eyes. They smiled at one another.

"I'm working on Stevie," she said. "It would be better if you had somebody who had had the lifetime fluency procedure.

"I know," Milton said. "I need a guinea pig."

E-mail from Brenda Bongiorno to Stefano Bongiorno:

You never got back to me about The Bookstore of Other Languages. It's a gold mine, I just know it is. Can't you just buy it from that guy? Pay him whatever he asks – you'll make ten times that the first year. Remember that if you do get it, I get a cut!

Brenda

E-mail from Mel Hanford to Brenda Bongiorno

Dear Brenda,

I'm just back from Roger's house. I can't believe my baby brother is seventy-one, mostly because I can't believe how hard I'm pushing eighty. But that's not why I'm writing.

Did you know that when Bryce went to help you in Albania, he had somehow bought an ability to speak Albanian? It's so weird! He told us about it at dinner. I should have known because he charged it to my card, but I had told him that I would pay for all the expenses and I was so upset I didn't pay close attention to the bills, I just paid them.

Also did you know that Bryce is engaged to a Frenchwoman? We heard all about that at dinner, and she was there, too. Very pleasant young woman and they seem very happy together. They haven't made any plans about getting married, though, because they can't figure out how and where they're going to live. Bryce, I think, would move to France except for the language. He could buy – he explained this to us – a lifetime of native speaking fluency at this strange place, The Bookstore of Other Languages, but he can't afford the hundred thousand dollars. I guess he's doing what he can to save money, but they'll both be pretty old by the time he has enough.

Here's my crazy idea. I was wondering if you might not be able to express your appreciation for the help that Bryce has given you by paying for him to have French for the rest of his life. Actually, Brenda, he's quite serious about this woman and it means a lot to him to be with her. I know it's a lot of money, but if your circumstances would allow it, it would make a great deal of difference to Bryce.

Just a thought.

Dad

E-mail from Stefano Bongiorno to Brenda Bongiorno:

I'm thinking about it. There are some problems. We need to know that the lifetime fluency procedure works. I offer you a deal. You do the procedure. If it works, I'll acquire the business and develop it. It will make a fortune and I'll give you one percent of the first year's gross.

Stevie

E-mail from Brenda Bongiorno to Stefano Bongiorno:

No way am I risking being your guinea pig! Why would I? But I'm working on finding you one. And no, I'm not taking one percent! I want five percent and I want it off the second year's gross.

Brenda

E-mail from Brenda Bongiorno to Bryce Hanford:

Dear Bryce,

It doesn't come easily to me to say this, but I have not treated you well. You rescued me in Albania not once, but twice. I don't know what would have happened to me if you had not helped me. And then, through you, I found The Bookstore of Other Languages. What a treasure it is! I plan to use them for all my travels in the future. Thank you for all you have done for me!

I had an e-mail from my father and that is really the reason I'm writing you. He tells me that you are engaged to a charming Frenchwoman. Congratulations! I'm very happy for you.

Bryce, I'd like to do something to thank you for all the trouble you have gone to on my behalf. Would you accept a gift? I understand from my father that you are saving up for the lifetime native-speaker fluency treatment at The Bookstore. It would be a pleasure for me to pay for that. Would you allow me to do that?

Your cousin,

Brenda

E-mail from Bryce Hanford to Brenda Bongiorno:

No thanks.

CHAPTER ELEVEN

"But, Bryce? Isn't that generous of her? What's the problem?"

"Brenda's the problem. Brenda doesn't have a generous bone in her body; she doesn't have a generous hair on her head, or, oh, I don't know, not a generous corpuscle in her veins."

"What are you worried about? The Bookstore wouldn't do it unless she had paid, would they? Are you thinking that you'd be stuck with the huge bill? Why would she do that?"

"No, that's not it, that's too easy to check up on. I just know that she is one hundred percent all for Brenda all the way, all the time. There has to be a catch."

Astrid poured them each a glass of wine, and brought his to him, kissing him first. She settled into the couch next to him.

"I hate it that spring vacation is over. I hate having to leave."

"I know. Me, too. I mean I hate it that you have to leave. When is your school year over?"

"Early July. Almost two months from now. I've lived so long without you, why is it so hard to be apart from you now?"

Bryce put an arm around her. "I know. Me, too. Listen, my love."

"Yes?"

"Your family has been in Rennes for a long time, yes? They know lots of people?"

She nodded and raised her eyebrows. "Yes, certainly. And?"

"I've been looking for jobs in that high-tech hub that you keep telling me about and not finding much. Do you think they'd be willing to ask around? Just be aware and let you know if they hear of anything?"

"Oh, yes, the family is very loyal. And you know, Mama has reported back to them faithfully. Or" – she hesitated – "if not faithfully, at least all in your favor."

"I don't even want to imagine."

"Also, Bryce, you know, there are schools in Rennes. It's a big city. I could look for a job there. I don't have to commit to anything, just look around."

"I don't see why not. I don't see much, though. God, this is hard!"

They drank their wine, each of them going over things in their own minds. They got up, went to the kitchen and worked silently, chopping and sautéing, roasting and basting. The silence finally caught up with them.

"Maybe I should take Brenda up on it. I'll think about it," he said.

E-mail from Bryce to Justin Goldsmith and Kendra Heglund:

How about I provide a tasty breakfast with coffee tomorrow, half an hour before opening? Let me know.

Once more they sat around Bryce's desk, glancing at one another uncertainly while Bryce passed out coffees and opened a box of pastries.

"Bryce, we get nervous when you buy breakfast," Kendra said. "Is everybody all right?"

Bryce smiled. "Yes, everybody is fine. Well, not me so much, but you already know everything about that."

"Oh," said Justin, "just the ordinary, everyday problem of how you're going to live the rest of your life with the woman you love. Just that problem?"

"Don't be smug, Justin, just because you've solved the problem for yourself."

Justin looked pleased. Kendra poked him and smiled indulgently.

"Children, behave yourselves."

They straightened up in their chairs.

"I need to make big changes; I need an escape route."

They looked puzzled.

"I don't see how I can stay on Eliza Island. If Astrid comes here, it will have to be Seattle. If she doesn't, then I go there. Either way, I have to be ready to move."

"That's . . . so . . . that will change everything," said Justin.

"What are you thinking about?" asked Kendra.

"I'm thinking about you. I have a proposal for you. What would you say to buying this business?"

They looked at one another, but couldn't say a word.

Bryce waved his arms. "Just listen to me. I've been thinking about it, and this may work out. Just hear me out and then go home and think about it. The way it works now is that I pay all the things I pay for, the rent and the inventory and the utilities, and so on; I pay you, and then I get to keep the rest. What if – just what if . . . what if we reversed it? You paid for everything and paid me first and then you got to keep the rest? We'd have to work out the price and God only knows what details – I haven't done this before. It would give me something to live on while I figured out what to do next."

They were speechless.

"Well, if you won't talk about it, will you think about it? Will you talk with somebody you trust who can advise you? Maybe there's even a parent whose advice would be helpful?"

Their words came in a rush. Yes, they would think about it, yes, it was very exciting, but oh, scary, too, and they had never thought about owning their own business, but they loved it here and they wanted to stay here and live here forever and raise their family here. At this point they suddenly became very quiet again and looked at the floor. Kendra's freckles disappeared as her face got very pink.

"Oh, my God!" cried Bryce. "Really?"

"Really!" said Justin, and there were many hugs and handshakes and smiles. Then it was time to clear up the last traces of breakfast and open for the day.

Bryce poured a glass of wine for Astrid and then for himself.

"They're going to do it."

"Oh, Bryce! And that means that you are going to do it!"

"Yeah, I know. I'm stunned. And a little afraid. It's like I'm jumping off a cliff. At least I'm jumping off with you. And speaking of jumping off cliffs . . . "

"Yes?"

"Kendra is pregnant."

"Oh, my! Well, that is a cliff."

They sat down to dinner. Even though it was May, throughout much of Astrid's visit, it had been chilly and drizzly, but today the sun had shone, gardens had come back to life, and a few brave souls had worn shorts and t-shirts.

"Speaking of even more cliffs," Bryce began.

"Yes?"

"We just have a couple of days left. Would you like to row around part of the island and see some petroglyphs? I can borrow Carlos's rowboat."

"Oh, yes!"

"Let's risk it tomorrow. We can take sandwiches and beer and have a picnic on the water."

The next day found them in a rowboat moving around the island, surrounded by glittering sunshine on the water. Bryce rowed past large houses with lawns and tennis courts, and then farther on to high, rocky cliffs, on an isolated island. At last they came to a deep narrow inlet, where they could move their boat in by pulling on the rocks. At the end the inlet widened, and there, on the flat sides of the cliff face, were dozens of wide-eyed faces, staring at them.

The boat rocked gently as Bryce threw a line around a rock. Astrid was silent, staring into the staring faces.

"I feel so exposed," she said. "All these faces."

Bryce said nothing.

She looked at him. "You're staring at me, too."

He adjusted his cushion and rearranged his legs.

"It's how I often feel when I'm with you," he said. "Exposed, but not in danger. Exposed and safe both."

Astrid stared again at the faces, stared back at Bryce, then looked away.

"Who made these?" she asked.

"I don't know. I've just read a little about them. They're Lushootseed, and the Lushootseed have been here a very very long time. These pictures could easily have been here a thousand years."

"Are they religious? Guardians? Hunting?"

"I don't know," he answered. "Those eyes with circles around them seem like searchlights, very . . . I don't know . . . confrontational and, I guess, spooky."

"I'm hungry all of a sudden," she said. "Want a sandwich? Do you think it would be sacrilegious to eat here? Or should we be doing some sort of ritual fasting?"

They ate their lunch under the surveillance of the ancient petroglyphs.

"I'm such a coward," she said suddenly.

"What?"

"I should have answered you before, and not changed the subject." She searched for words. "It's easy to watch other people, especially easy to want to know about you. I want to know all about you." Astrid reached into her pocket, pulled out a tissue, and wiped her eyes.

"Astrid! What? What is it?"

"Oh, it's just that it's so hard to be known. Even these faces carved in the rock make me want to hide. I'll take the listener role, the observer role, every time. Just as long as I don't have to show who I am."

"I don't understand. You're wonderful."

"No. No, I'm not. I live with my mother. I spend my life trying to convince high-school girls that they truly need to understand history. I read. And the one time I let myself go, I married a man who complained when I had cancer that I was neglecting him and wound up finding my body disgusting and telling me so and leaving me. What was I thinking? How could I have been so stupid as not to see who he was? I who am so observant!"

Bryce moved toward her and the boat rocked alarmingly.

"Astrid! Don't do this to yourself!"

She wiped her eyes again, and blew her nose.

"Here's the bizarre part. I see that I've made these mistakes, and I tell myself that I'm a mess and a coward. And then I look at Marina, who is so free and brave and adventurous, and I admire her and love her, but there's no fortune big enough that would pay me to change my life for hers. Isn't that ridiculous?"

"No. Not one little bit ridiculous. Just very lucky for me."

They backed the boat out of the inlet, and rowed back toward the town. They didn't speak, each following their own thoughts. As they approached the harbor, Bryce pulled in his oars, and they floated freely."

"Astrid," he began, then stopped. "Astrid," he began again, "why didn't you meet me at the Eiffel Tower my last day in Paris?"

"From the day I met you I wasn't afraid of your knowing me, and it scared me to death."

That evening, while Astrid made dinner, Bryce wrote Brenda. E-mail from Bryce Hanford to Brenda Bongiorno:

Okay. I'll do it.

Bryce

Astrid was gone. Again. Each time seemed more painful, Bryce thought as he tried to settle into his day at work. He was reading through his e-mails when his phone rang.

"Bryce? Stevie."

"Stevie! Hello!"

"Bryce, I have to bring you up to date on a few things. Did you know, has Brenda told you, that I'm thinking about buying The Bookstore of Other Languages?"

"No! I had no idea."

"I've been holding off because the owner can't guarantee his lifetime fluency procedure. Now Brenda tells me that you are volunteering to have it done. What's going on?"

"I thought she was paying the hundred thousand for me."

"Brenda? Pay? Bryce, what are you thinking?"

"You're right. I wanted to believe it. I should have known better."

"Bryce, forget it. You can't do it. Milton is a fraud."

"He can't be a fraud! It works! Stevie, I've done this thing five times, and it works. Where's the fraud?"

"Milton's the fraud. He almost killed somebody in Netherlands trying out this contraption. "

"Stevie, listen to me. I'm going to do this. I'm in love. I love this woman so much, I'd . . . I don't know . . . I'd abdicate my throne for her. And I'm going to get lifetime fluency in French for her. I've helped you bail Brenda out twice. You owe me!"

In June, Bryce once more made the long trip into Seattle for a medical procedure. It wasn't the terrifying trip he had made for the lump in the throat, but a familiar process, what he thought would probably be a repetition of his previous five visits. Once more he drove off the freeway and down toward the harbor, parking in a block with weeds in the sidewalks and broken bottles in the gutter.

The hand-painted plastic sidewalk sign with was still there, scratched and faded. He walked in and stopped suddenly. All the books were gone. The bookcases were gone and the floors were swept clean. There was no sign of Blythe with the moon and sun earrings or the radiant Cilla with the stylish corn rows. Bryce walked to office at the back of the store, looked in and saw blonde, stocky Dr. Milton, in black jeans, black t-shirt, and black leather motorcycle jacket, still looking like Brad Pitt. Milton was leaning over the desk, looking at the computer screen and talking with a man seated at the desk, a man that Bryce didn't recognize, a balding, middle-aged, Asian man. Boxes of files sat on the desk and on the floor. Bryce tapped on the door frame. Milton looked up.

"Oh, good morning, Mr. Hanford."

"Uh, hello. What's happening here? Are we going ahead with the procedure?"

Milton's head bobbed. "Oh, yes. We're just in the middle of moving. Actually, we're, expanding. I don't remember if we met. I'm Dr. Daniel Milton. This is my . . . business associate, Dr. Goh."

"Hello, Mr. Hanford. Actually, I'm a business associate of Mr. Bongiorno's. I believe you know him."

"I do indeed."

Milton glanced at Goh, then back at Bryce. "It's very exciting that you've decided to have the lifetime native-speaker fluency! We'll get right to it. If you would just sign this release . . ." He reached into one of the file boxes for the familiar form. Bryce bent over the desk and signed it.

Milton cleared his throat. "Let's go next door, shall we?" Dr. Goh gestured meaningfully at the papers on the desk. "If you'd just sign here, Dr. Milton, before you leave?"

Milton looked surprised. "I thought we were going to wait until after the procedure," he said."

Goh looked at him firmly. "As you know, if you have read these agreements, they cover all contingencies. Please sign."

Milton shrugged, sat at the desk, frowned, and scribbled his name.

Dr. Milton and Dr. Goh walked with Bryce back to the street and next door to the free clinic, where they entered and went down the hallway. Milton opened the door on the left and there was Cilla wearing a lab coat over a pale pink dress, smiling, beautiful as always.

"Ready?" said Milton.

Bryce sat in the familiar reclining chair and looked around the familiar room.

Milton picked up a bottle of pills. "You know that the lifetime native-fluency procedure takes longer than the others?"

"Yes, I understand," said Bryce.

"Good. And I really do recommend a sedative. It will wear off quickly and you'll be able to drive home with no trouble."

"Well, if you think so . . ."

"Really, it would be much better. Here you go, just this one pill. Cilla, a glass of water? Mr. Hanford, what music would you like today? You like classical? Bach cello suites, or maybe the Mozart flute and harp concerto? The Mozart? Fine."

As Bryce listened to the flowing conversation between the flute and harp, he felt his muscles relaxing, and then he dozed.

As Bryce, surrounded by Milton, Goh, and Cilla, slept in the reclining chair, the door opened and Stevie quietly stood at the back of the room.

Dr. Goh stepped forward. "Mr. Milton, we understand that this procedure has never been done before. As you also know, we're aware of the incident at the University of Leiden. Please tell us once more about what precautions you have taken to assure Mr. Hanford's safety."

Milton frowned. "That 'incident,' as you call it, happened sixteen years ago. Since then, I've refined the procedure so that it works every time. You know that yourself – you underwent the procedure with perfect results, exactly as guaranteed, with no side effects at all. The only reason we haven't done the lifetime fluency before is the lack of a customer. I don't anticipate any problem at all," Milton answered.

He nodded to Cilla, who lifted and unfolded a device from a cabinet built in to the back of the chair, and carefully strapped a helmet-like cap around Bryce's head. Milton plugged a USB cable into a port on the apparatus, connecting it with a computer on a fold-out table on one arm of the chair. Various monitors brightened. Dr. Goh took out a notebook and began writing in it.

"As you see," Milton said, "we position a magnetic coil over the left frontal lobe, first over Broca's area and then over Wernicke's area." He continued to describe the process in an instructive manner as he manipulated the coil and directed it by typing into the computer. Bryce continued to breathe easily and appeared relaxed. Dr. Goh continued to observe closely, make notes, and ask occasional questions. Unnoticed by Milton, Stevie was recording everything with his phone.

Milton's audience watched him for over an hour as he checked things off a list and entered numbers on a form, making frequent modifications in the coil and on the computer. At almost two hours into the operation, Milton reached over and adjusted a nob on the cap. Bryce screamed and his whole body became rigid. Milton stood up and looked around wildly.

"I don't know what to do!" he said, "This has never happened before!" Bryce's body began to shake.

"Get out of my way!" Dr. Goh cried, and pushing Milton aside, reached over and put his hand on Bryce's chest. "He's having a seizure! Call 9-1-1!"

"No! Nobody call! They might bring the police," cried Milton.

"Call now!"

Cilla reached in the pocket of her lab coat and took out her phone. Milton saw her, swung an arm around and knocked her to the ground. The phone fell on the floor. Stevie jumped across the room, backhanded Milton into the wall, and picked up the phone. He turned to Goh.

"Call now!" Goh ordered.

"Damn!" cried Stevie and punched in 9-1-1.

As Stevie gave information to the emergency service, Milton pulled himself off the floor. He grabbed Dr. Goh and pulled him away from Bryce, who then fell from the chair onto the floor, hitting his head with an audible crack. Stevie dropped the phone and heaved Milton aside, while Goh stripped off his lab coat, took coats from every one and piled them on Bryce to keep him warm. Cilla picked herself up and groped her way to a chair.

Soon, sirens wailed, brakes screeched, and uniforms poured through the door. EMTs surrounded Bryce, who lay unconscious on the floor, his head in a pool of blood. As Bryce was carried out on a stretcher, two paramedics questioned Stevie and Goh. Stevie turned to bring Milton into the conversation, but by that time, Milton was far away.

CHAPTER TWELVE

Letter from Dr. Benedict Goh to Ms. Cilla Mitchell, registered mail

Dear Ms. Mitchell,

I was glad to see when we last met that you had recovered from last month's events. Your efforts were heroic and very possibly helped save Mr. Hanford's life.

We recognize that you are an experienced employee, and that your expertise will be valuable in our future business expansion. Thus, we are prepared to offer you a six-month paid leave of absence at your current salary, whether or not you choose to work with us in the future. When we open to the public, should you choose to return, I am prepared to offer you a more secure position, which will include health insurance and a pension plan.

When we met, you were willing to discuss with me the circumstances under which you would forego a civil suit against Daniel Milton and against The Bookstore of Other Languages, now owned by Bongiorno Enterprises. This letter lists our responses to your concerns:

Your concern for Ms. Blythe Parsons is understandable, and I can assure you that she has been offered similar benefits to those that you have been offered. It is entirely possible that you would be co-workers once more, but under more favorable circumstances.

Mr. Hanford is currently in a coma at St. Olaf Hospital in Seattle. Doctors there tell me that while he may recover fully, they cannot be sure, and it remains to be seen what language abilities he might have acquired, and also what side effects might have developed in the course of his "treatment."

LOQUELA, LLC has assumed all liability for Mr. Hanford's medical bills. Of course we plan to offer him a substantial settlement as well.

Neither the police nor the FBI have been able so far to locate Daniel Milton.

I hope, Ms. Mitchell, you will consider working with us. Unlike "Dr." Milton, I have legitimate degrees, including an MD from the Johns Hopkins University School of Medicine and am board certified in Neurology; I also have a PhD in pharmacology an MBA.

I want you to know, also, that I and my research staff from Bongiorno Pharmaceuticals have completely redesigned Milton's apparatus and reprogrammed his procedure. We measured the results by doing the procedure on ourselves, acquiring native fluency in several languages. We are now busy preparing to open language clinics in six cities in the United States, with more to come. We anticipate that LOQUELA, LLC will become a highly successful international business.

LOQUELA,LLC. would welcome your participation. Should you wish to join us, please review and sign the enclosed contract and non-disclosure agreement and return to me.

I look forward to working with you in the future.
Best wishes,
Benedict Goh, MD, PhD
CEO, LOQUELA, LLC
CC: Stefano Bongiorno, Sean Declan Murphy, Attorney-at-law

Bryce was in the Picasso Museum. He tried to walk up the broad staircase, but he never got to the top. It was like an escalator that just kept going and going and never got anywhere. He opened his eyes and saw a portrait of Jacqueline Roque, looking tender and concerned. He smiled and closed his eyes, but the museum was no longer there, just a warm darkness.

"He opened his eyes! He did, but just for a second."

"That's a very good sign. You know, coma patients can take some time to come around. They don't just sit up and take up where they left off. But this is very good."

He heard whispers and the odd thing was that they sounded like the whispers of his parents. How silly. He smiled.

"Oh, Roger! He smiled!"

"Bryce! Bryce! Are you there?"

"Don't be silly, Roger, of course he's there. Bryce! Can you hear us?"

Of course he heard them. Why wouldn't he hear them? He slept.

"He doesn't look so bad. He looks like you could just tell him to get the hell out of bed, get some clothes on, and come out for a beer."

"He looks god-awful. Look at those stitches in his head. Sheesh!"

Bryce opened his eyes. "Ginnie. Ashley. What are you doing here?"

"Hello, Bryce." Ginnie's long purple curl dangled over his nose. "We're here because we came to see you."

"Where's here?"

"You're in the hospital, what do you think?"

"Ginnie?"

"Yes?"

"Do you think you could call someone?"

"You want a doctor or a nurse or Astrid?"

"Astrid! What's happening?"

"That's what a lot of us would like to know."

This was too hard. Time to go back to sleep.

When he woke up some time later, he found that he was indeed dressed in a hospital gown and lying in a hospital bed, hooked up to an IV and God knows what else. There was a person sitting in a chair next to the bed, and that person was Astrid.

"Astrid."

"Bryce."

"I love you."

"I know. I love you, too."

"What happened?"

"What do you remember?"

"Mozart. No, Bach. Oh – Dr. Milton! Oh – am I speaking French or anglais?"

"English right now."

"How did I wind up aquí?"

"It's something of a puzzle."

"What do you know?"

"The best we can figure out is that you had a seizure at The Bookstore and then fell on the floor and cracked your head. Then Dr. Milton disappeared. A young woman, Cilla, was here and told me about it."

"Cilla? She's from the knjižara. What was she doing here?"

"She came to see how you were doing and we talked a bit. It's all very confusing, but it seems that the Bookstore has been bought by somebody related to your cousin Brenda. You meant 'Bookstore,' right?"

"Brenda! Did Uncle Mel buy the Bookstore? Of course I meant Bookstore. This is so verwirrend."

"We can talk about it later. But what I do want you to know is that all your hospital bills are being paid by a company called LOQUELA, but it seems to be owned by Stevie. Who is Stevie?"

"This really is too much."

"Maybe we could not talk for a while, but maybe you could hold my hand?"

Astrid arrived at the hospital a few days later, and walked into Bryce's room to find two strangers there looking at Bryce, a tall, gray-haired, well-tailored man and a shorter, balding Asian man. As she walked into the room, they turned, and the tall man addressed her.

"Ms. Ollivier?"

"Yes?" she answered.

"I'm Bryce's former cousin-in-law, Stefano Bongiorno, that is, Stevie. This is Dr. Benjamin Goh, a business associate. Could we have a word with you?"

"I would very much like to have a word with you," she replied.

Stevie glanced at Bryce, lying still in his hospital bed. "Perhaps we could find a quiet place to talk?"

"There's a conference room down the hall. Let's try that."

They sat around the table. No one wanted to start the conversation. Finally, Stevie cleared his throat and began. "Ms. Ollivi . . ." but Astrid interrupted him, and weeks of repressed anger exploded within her.

"How dare you come here!" Astrid cried. "Look at Bryce, look at what you've done to him! You should be ashamed of yourself! Bryce came to you for help and what did you do? He may never recover!" Astrid found herself weeping. "And he did it for me," she said, miserably, and then simply sobbed.

Hospital conference rooms are amply supplied with tissues, and after some time Astrid mopped her face, then looked severely at Stevie. "Well, what do you have to say for yourself?" she asked.

"Ms. Ollivier. Dr. Goh and I came here hoping to tell Bryce, but we will tell you instead, that indeed, we are ashamed. What has happened to Bryce is unforgivable, and we don't hope for your forgiveness. What we do hope for is to offer as much compensation as we can."

Astrid sniffed and blew her nose. "What can you possibly do?"

"I am a businessman. Over much time and in many situations I have considered what people owe and what they are owed."

"Well?"

Stevie smiled, a little grimly. "I have known Bryce for a long time. He could hardly be more different from his cousin, my former wife. If it were Brenda, the minute she came out of a coma, she'd be on the phone with her lawyer. I doubt it will occur to Bryce. Of course, he could call a lawyer, but he won't need to, because I think I would give him anything he asked for."

Astrid listened and watched Stevie silently, and he began to feel the effects of her careful, patient observation, the effects that had so moved Bryce when he first met her.

Stevie ran his hand through his thick, salt-and-pepper curls, and continued. "I haven't brought any legal documents for you or Bryce to read and sign, but I do have this for you. He put his hand in his inside jacket pocket and pulled out an envelope.

"It's Bryce's. No strings. You can open it."

Astrid opened the envelope and opened her eyes wide as she saw the number printed on the check.

"We're not done. We're working hard on developing the new business and making the procedures safe and effective. We'll want to know about Bryce's progress, and if and when there's more we can do to help, we'll be there. "

Later Astrid showed Bryce Stevie's check. "So, there's one thing we won't have to worry about. Now, just rest and get better."

Bryce was not to get the rest he needed, at least that night. Just after dinner, Merle Haggard's voice announced a call from Linda.

"Mom! What's happening?"

"Oh, Bryce, I'm sorry to call you and of course you don't have to do anything about it, but you just won't believe this."

"What, Mom?"

"Your Uncle Mel is here. Brenda is missing again."

The deck of Brenda Bongiorno's Cancun apartment looked out over the beach. Wrapped in a silk-lined, sequined, zebra-striped bathrobe, Brenda lingered over a cup of coffee, her newly manicured fingers tapping the glass table. From inside, someone turned off the shower, and in a few moments, Daniel Milton, a towel wrapped around him, opened the screen door and bent over to kiss her.

"I've been thinking about what's next," she said.

"Oddly enough, I've been thinking about what's next and also where's next," he said, sitting down and helping himself to a croissant.

"You tell me what and where and I'll set up the business end of it."

"The world is big. Who doesn't want to learn English without trying? I could set that up without thinking twice. But I hate to limit TMS to language. There's so much money to be made by connecting the body to the brain."

"What are you thinking about?"

"What would you say to enhanced sex drive?"

"Oh, my God in heaven. You can do that?"

"Why not?"

"Where?"

Milton thought. "I'm thinking about Brazil."

By early July, Bryce and Astrid were sitting on the deck of his house, looking out over the trees to the water.

"And ahora I'm rich."

"You certainly are," said Astrid. "Well, it depends on what you call rich, but I imagine a nice comfortable five million dollars might keep you afloat for the time being."

"Yes. Keep us afloat. Yes, I think so."

They sat on the deck and looked at the clouds.

"Astrid – tell me noch einmal. Porqué am I rich?"

"I don't really understand what happened. You went in for the lifetime native-speaker French treatment. Something dreadful happened, and again, I don't know what it was, but you had a seizure and hit your head and fractured your skull. I only got here afterwards. I can't find anybody from your Bookstore, nobody answers the phone or answers e-mail, and the building is empty. Besides, I've been more worried about you than about the Bookstore, so I don't know what happened. When I got here I made sure that you were alive, and I talked with your doctors and found that you were probably going to get better, I was so relieved I couldn't think about anything else. But then, I came to, and thought to talk to the hospital about medical bills, and they told me that they were being paid, and it was LOQUELA, and it turns out that that is Stevie. Then I talked with Stevie and he gave me the check.

"I'm so deurmekaar."

"Bryce, this is scary. You keep using words that I don't know. Sometimes they're French, but most of the time I don't know if you're making the words up or if they're words from other languages. I'm worried."

"Je ne peux penser about it now."

Bryce drifted. He took long walks, some with Astrid, others alone. He returned to the garden project, he read books and took naps. He felt as if he were floating downstream, with no goal in mind other than delighting in being with Astrid.

One day in mid-July they were sitting on the deck off the back of the house, looking over the raised beds in the back yard, now neatly surrounded by a deer-proof fence. It occurred to him that she must have arrived during the school year.

"Did you quit your job?" he asked.

"No," she replied. "I took a leave of absence. They didn't want to let me take it, but I convinced them that we were married in the States, so then they did let me take it, but they're not very happy with me. Anyway, now school is over for the year. I'll have to tell them soon whether I want to come back or not."

"And what about Justin and Kendra?"

"They've been running the shop with no help from you, and they said to tell you that they accept your offer. Whatever that is."

"Oh, that's very goed. I'm going to sälja them the business."

"Really? The things I don't know! And there it is again!"

"What?"

"You're going to sell them the business?"

"Yes, that's what I said."

"Not quite. You know, you keep using words from all kinds of languages and I don't think you know you're doing it. We need to see a doctor."

"I'm pretty tired of liječnici right now. Give me a few mas weeks. Maybe I'll récupérer by myself."

Astrid sighed. "And speaking of Kendra, she is looking exceptionally blooming. Is she?"

"Is she what?"

"Blooming?"

"Now that you remind me, I think that she is indeed blooming."

Bryce took another look at the raised beds.

"It's juillet," he said. "Is it too late to plant vegetales?"

"I don't know. I'm a city girl. But speaking of calendars, do you know what today is?" asked Astrid.

"Actually, no I don't. Woensdag? Thursday?"

"It's Wednesday, but more to the point, it's July 14."

"Bastille Day!"

"You haven't forgotten all your history."

Bryce was silent. He looked at her thoughtfully.

"Astrid."

"That would be me, the very me, the person that I am."

"We have dinero."

"Money."

"That's what I said."

She looked at him with concern.

"We could do etwas outrageous."

"Get married in France?"

"That, certainly."

"You mean go live in Tasmania or Martinique. Do something like Marina would do?"

Bryce laughed. "Nein. You and I will never be like Marina. I was thinking of doing something more like you or I, being the persone that we are, would do. If we wanted to, we could both ophouden our jobs and go back to escuela. We could really study Geschichte."

Astrid looked across the garden to the mountains in the distance.

"That's a new possibility – a little overwhelming, but I can imagine it. I'll think about it. You would want to study history?"

"What an aufregend question. I'll have to think that one over. And over. But right off the top of my confused höfuð, I think architectural history. You could get your doctorate. "

"It's dizzying to think about."

"Or even, well, I don't mean to push any louco ideas . . ."

"Are you thinking of our doing some blooming of our own?"

"Maybe. If you wouldn't rule it out."

Astrid bit her lip and shook her head. "It's too much to think about all at once. Maybe. I don't know. I'm afraid to even hope. And, you know, I did have chemotherapy. I'd have to talk with my doctors."

"I understand."

"But now I want to change the subject."

"Yes?"

"How would you feel if Mama came to visit?"

"Really? That would be meraviglioso!"

He thought a minute.

"That is, I think it would be wonderful. What would she do about Tabak?"

Astrid winced, but carried on. "You know, she is very tired of lounging around the house, and imagining that she's ill, and her boredom with home and curiosity about our world here is pushing her to try a patch. I'm trying not to hope that she would give up nicotine entirely – that would be too wonderful. What I really think is that she is scheming to meet Dr. Martini."

"He's a goner. Where will she stay? This maison is so small."

"We could get her a B&B. Even if it is summer, we might be able to afford it."

"We can afford a lot maintenant. If she's up for it, I'm up for it."

"Good. I seem to be all over the place today. There's so much we've not been able to talk about."

"What's the next thing?"

"I keep wondering if you really do have the lifetime fluency in French. For the rest of your life. The weird words that pop up really worry me. But also - can you speak French?"

"I don't know. I don't know how to change gears. And "Doctor" Milton isn't here to show me how. It makes me tan cansado to think about it. Let me see. I think I'll try domani."

"I'll write Mama," Astrid said. "I'll have to figure out what and how much to explain to her!"

"What you don't tell her, she'll figure out," Bryce advised.

By August, Bryce was feeling much better. He had more energy and his head was much clearer, although his vocabulary continued to be an international patchwork of words. He had gone back to work, but mostly in order to ease the transition for Justin and Kendra from employees to owners, which he had arranged on the easiest possible terms for them. Justin and Kendra stepped into their new roles hesitantly at first, and then, appropriately for a couple taking on family responsibilities, with more confidence. Their first decision as co-owners was to take on Odell, a scrawny kid who had been taking computers apart since kindergarten and putting them back together since fourth grade. Odell had taught himself programming, but couldn't get all that excited about college. He was pleased to get a job doing what he already knew what to do, where he would learn more. Kendra, in increasing bloom, continued to greet the customers, sort out those needing repairs, and gracefully persuading them to explain in detail the problems they were having.

After much second-guessing, Astrid had taken the momentous step of officially quitting her teaching job. Once she had written the school, she was rewarded with a wave of relief, convincing her that she had taken the right step. As for the future, neither Bryce nor Astrid had come to a decision. They were together, he was recovering, and that was more than enough.

On a clear, warm August morning, Bryce and Astrid took first one ferry, then another, and drove to Sea-Tac to welcome her mother to America.

They waited for her at the baggage claim area and were finally rewarded with the sight of Thérèse, laughing with two expensively-suited American men, and teasing them about their French. She eventually noticed Bryce and Astrid and trotted over to them in ridiculously high heels.

"Oh, my dears!" she cried and embraced and kissed them both. Bryce was pleased to see that he had been promoted to four cheek kisses. She pointed out two hefty suitcases on the carousel, and he bent over to grab them as they passed by. He got one, but missed the other and had to wait for it to come around again. While he was waiting an arm waved in front of him and a voice whispered in his ear – "the red one is mine. Grab it, too, will you?"

"Marina!"

His cry of astonishment brought Thérèse and a surprised Astrid.

"Thérèse wasn't sure about traveling alone – not that she stays alone for very long – and I thought I might as well come, too, and pay my visit to Doctor Martini."

With a bit of hesitation, and for the first time since coming out of his coma, Bryce moved unsteadily into French. They took their bags and made their way up escalators, over a sky bridge, and up in an elevator to where the car was parked. All the way, Thérèse told stories about her long flight, the dreadfulness of Charles de Gaulle airport, the dreadfulness of the Atlanta airport, the charm of her seatmate – she had his name and e-mail address – and the incompetence of the flight attendants, while Marina added to and corrected the stories, only occasionally arguing with her. Bryce needed only to listen and to understand and make an occasional grunt of compre-hension. It wasn't until they were at the car that Thérèse caught her breath, stopped talking, and lit a cigarette.

As Bryce explained to Thérèse that she couldn't smoke in the car, he thought he was speaking French, but he couldn't be sure. Thérèse pouted and unwrapped a stick of nicotine gum and put it in her mouth.

"Oh, well. Americans." She shrugged.

Bryce opened the back door for Astrid and Marina, and the front passenger door for Thérèse, who got in and adjusted her skirt, pulled down the mirror and renewed her lipstick.

"What a pretty car," said Marina. "Is it new?"

"New for us," Bryce said. "You know that we've come into some money – it's a long Geschichte and I'll tell you the whole story later. We plan to be very cuidadoso with the money, but we did allow ourselves to get a newish used car. My old one was pretty lagunenud."

Thérèse turned to look at him. "What?"

Astrid, in the back seat, whispered to Marina, "Oh, my goodness. Now he's doing it with French. I'll tell you later."

They drove up the interstate toward Seattle.

"But, Mama, now that you have complained, tell us how your flight really was."

"Oh, not so bad. Before the flight I met a man in the airport bar and he was on the same flight and had a word with the cap-tain, or somebody, and I got a seat in first class. No – don't look at me that way. You know I'm not well and it made a great difference to me! Yes, Marina had to sit in coach, but she is young."

They went down a hill and Seattle appeared in the distance.

"The Emerald City," said Bryce.

"Why do they call it that? It looks like any city – no color."

"You'll see. It's a little joke, you know, about the movie 'The Tovenaar of Oz.' But, really, Seattle is very green. Not vert like environmentally careful, although it is certainly that. It's because of all the trees and other plants. It's green because of all the mmiri ozuzo."

"What?"

"What?" asked Bryce.

Marina returned to St. Olaf Hospital with her entourage. They met Katy Bunch, who greeted them pleasantly and led Marina away for her exam. The rest of them waited in the oncology lobby, Astrid and Bryce reading, while Thérèse examined the paintings on the wall and then moved to the windows with views of the waterfront. She looked around the city, into the busy streets, and then out to the Olympic Mountains. Then back to the streets to see how people were dressed.

A white-coated man looked through the waiting room and found Astrid.

"Ah, there you are!" said Dr. Martini, in French. "How happy I am to see you again. Happy, too, to report that your – is it really your niece? – is doing very well."

"Dr. Martini! What a pleasure."

"Bryce! How good to see you. And to report to you that Marina is doing very well." They shook hands.

He looked from one to the other. "You know," he said, frowning thoughtfully, "that in medical school, we are trained to be very careful observers. It is that training that leads me to comment on rings on your fingers. Are congratulations in order?"

They assured him that they were indeed in order, and in the midst of their conversation, another voice was heard – "C'est le médecin?"

Dr. Martini looked around to find an older, slightly curvier version of Astrid, with enormous blue eyes batting black eyelashes. "Mais, oui!" he said to her.

"You did not tell me that Dr. Martini spoke French," she said to Bryce and Astrid accusingly.

"Dr. Martini," began Bryce, "this is Mme. Thérèse Ollivier, Marina's . . . step-great-aunt?"

"We won't talk about it that way, Bryce," scolded Thérèse.

Marina joined them and eventually succeeded in helping them to detach Thérèse and Dr. Martini, and to go out and be tourists in Seattle.

They began at the Space Needle, eating lunch and watching as the city of Seattle seemed to orbit around them. They spoke in French, and to Bryce it was becoming effortless, although there were words he used that the others didn't understand, which he found perplexing.

"Shall we go to the Pike Street Market?" asked Marina. "How can you say you've visited Seattle and not gone to the market?"

"We can, but I have someplace I want to visit first," said Bryce. They got in the car, and Bryce drove down the hill toward the waterfront, navigating the one-way streets, and finally pulling up to a dingy block near the viaduct.

"There it is," he said.

"There is what?" they asked.

There was nothing. An empty storefront. Most of the shops that had been there before were gone, and others had taken their place – a nail salon, used musical instruments. The free clinic was there, but Bryce was willing to bet that the room on the left down the hallway was put to different use now. Where was the beautiful Cilla, the pixie-ish Blythe?

"It was a bookstore," he said, looking at Astrid. "It's the place where I learned French. It was a very dziwny place."

"I believe you," she said. "I suppose."

"What has happened to it?" asked Marina.

"I don't know," he answered. And they continued on to the Pike Street Market, where all tourists must go.

Late that evening, with Thérèse and Marina safely tucked into their B&B, Astrid decided that the conversation about Bryce's speech couldn't be put off any longer.

"Bryce," she said, "I want you to call Stevie."

He raised his eyebrows. "Why?"

"You're physically much better, I would say you're well, but you can't live the rest of your life speaking randomly in a dozen languages."

"I know it sounds crazy, but I hate to bother Stevie."

"I don't. It's time."

The next day, Bryce called. The stern voice answered, and Stevie was on the line.

"Stevie, I'm calling you, well, really because apparently you talked with Astrid when I was in the hospital, and now she wants me to call you. You've already given me five million dollars. It seems to me that you've done everything you can. But I'm stuck. It seems to me that I'm well. But there is a side-effect that's not going away. Stevie, I don't realize I'm doing it, but I'm using words from all kinds of different languages."

"Bryce," Stevie answered. "You know that I am first a businessman. You must have guessed that I have connections that are not entirely . . . well, that run . . . let's say . . . parallel to the law. This doesn't mean that I'm lawless or lacking in principles. My principles are my principles, and I honor them. As I see it, you got into this purely through helping the family. You did nothing wrong, you took great pains, you suffered through dealing with Brenda. This I honor. I should never have allowed you to undergo the procedure that harmed you, and I'd like to make things right for you now – completely right, as far as I can. If you want to look at it another way, let's talk about a different principal – I feel as if I owe you, and I never like to owe or to be owed. So, let's do something."

"Stevie, I don't know what to say. Say you could help. How would that work? What would you do?"

"Let me talk it over with Dr. Goh. We'll get back to you."

For Thérèse and Marina's farewell dinner, Astrid and Bryce took them ferry-hopping to a neighboring island. At La Valenciana, they sat for hours enjoying the time together as they watched the sun set over the harbor and savored the seafood, saffron rice, and a chilled dry rosé. Bryce and Marina each suffered some slight feelings of guilt, remembering the sequel to their last dinner there, but quickly suppressed them. Thérèse was in great spirits.

"I never thought I would travel so far and enjoy it so much!" she said. "It's so beautiful here, and I'm almost willing to say that I'm in good health!"

"Good health suits you, maman," said Astrid. "You look more beautiful than ever."

Bryce looked across the table. "Marina, you seem pensive. It's unlike you."

Marina took a sip of wine and looked out over the boats in the harbor. "It's true. I'm sad to leave. Also I have come to a great decision."

She had their attention.

"Before I left Rennes, I had a conversation with a man I've known for many years, Yann Madec, Dr. Madec. He's a pediatrician. He asked me a question, and I have to figure out the answer before I return."

Three people stopped breathing.

"Well?" asked Astrid.

Marina answered, but in a whisper so soft they couldn't hear her.

"Well?" asked Bryce.

"Well," Marina said in a louder voice, "I'm going to say yes."

Bryce gestured to the waitress and ordered a bottle of champagne.

CHAPTER THIRTEEN

South Lake Union in Seattle has gone from an abandoned industrial area to the newest high-tech and hip neighborhood, complete with glass-clad office buildings, new restaurants fusing the latest foods, a brand-new lakeside park, and an adorable trolley. South Lake Union was the inevitable site for the flagship office of the latest in high-tech wonders, LOQUELA, LLC., now open in Seattle, and soon to open clinics in six more cities in the U.S. and then around the globe. LOQUELA's breakthrough technology using transcranial magnetic stimulation in combination with a highly secret computer program, made it possible for ordinary people to acquire fluency in any language at various levels, and for various lengths of time. Its most astonishing offering was a lifetime of native-speaker ability, available for a mere million dollars. Executives from international businesses, from coffee merchants to biotech firms, were lining up for procedures that would take them from Seoul to Stockholm, Rome to Sydney. LOQUELA also provided personal business coaches, who would counsel the executives in local customs and etiquette.

In early December Bryce and Astrid presented themselves at the imposing opaque glass counter in the lobby and asked for Dr. Benedict Goh. The receptionist widened her eyes at an appointment with someone of such eminence, made a call, and said "Dr. Goh's assistant will meet you on the eleventh floor."

In the elevator cage, a translucent glass cylinder, Bryce felt as if he were being swept up into another world. The elevator stopped, the doors opened, and there was the ever-luminous Cilla.

"Mr. Hanford! I'm so glad to see you! And you look very much better than the last time I saw you!"

"Cilla! It's you! Oh . . . Cilla, this is my wife, Astrid Ollivier." They shook hands.

"Please come this way."

She led him into an office with a view to the north, where Mount Baker shone in the distance. To the west gleamed Elliott Bay and the faraway Olympic range, covered in snow.

The Chinese gentleman at the desk rose, greeted Astrid in a courtly manner, and introduced himself to Bryce. They had just seated themselves when Cilla appeared again. "Dr. Goh? Mr. Bongiorno is here," and Stevie walked into the room, closing the door behind him.

There followed a long discussion, in which Bryce and Astrid learned about Nicolaas Kruse and his disastrous academic career. Dr. Goh explained how he was able to build on Kruse's invention, bringing in a cadre of neuropsychologists and medical engineers, who were able to evaluate the procedure, erase its faulty pathways, and build new and better highways to language fluency. The new programs had been tested, made available to the public and were wildly successful. Bongiorno Enterprises expected to transform international business.

"I see that Cilla is içi. What about Blythe?" asked Bryce.

Stevie explained that because of their experience with Milton, they had been invaluable sources of information, if not technical, then practical. Both of them were now trusted employees of LOQUELA.

"And what about mich?" Bryce asked faintly, looking from Stevie to Dr. Goh.

Dr. Goh cleared his throat. "We understand that you are having side effects from your treatment. Considering who did the treatment, we are not surprised; but we are concerned and would like to make amends to you beyond the financial settlement that we have already offered. In fact, we would like to correct the situation. Mr. Hanford, we understand that you might be reluctant to undergo another treatment. Since your terrifying experience in June we have done dozens of successful native-fluency procedures, beginning with doing the experiments on ourselves. Would you consider it again, but this time the right way?"

Bryce looked at Astrid and saw love, but no answer.

"Dr. Goh," Bryce said, "Stevie? Would you please excuse us and let me have a word with Astrid?"

"Certainly," said Dr. Goh, who rose from his desk, and left the room with Stevie.

"Astrid," Bryce began. "I insisted on doing this before, and look where it got me. If I insistir on doing it ancora, will you still love me?"

Astrid nodded, speechless.

"Because," Bryce continued, "burtséð, what really counts is that in some very fundamental way that je don't begin to comprendre, Du und ich speak the same language, and nada will ever change that."

They stood for a moment in close embrace and then opened the door to the hallway where Stevie and Goh were waiting.

"Let's do it," said Bryce.

And so, Stevie took Astrid out for a long and lavish lunch, astonishing her with his knowledge of Gilbert and Sullivan operettas. She in turn wound up comparing late Victorian London to Belle Époque Paris. In the meantime, Dr. Goh put Bryce through a battery of tests, confirming some possibilities, eliminating others. Stevie brought Astrid back to LOQUELA in time for her to join Bryce in the procedure room.

"Are you still ready to go through with this?" she asked Bryce.

"Oui. Yes, I have to. What did you and Stevie talk about at pranzo?"

"I talked and talked and talked. I think it was all nerves, but I think we talked about Offenbach and Edwardian music halls."

"Are you ready?" asked Dr. Goh.

And once more and he hoped for the last time, Bryce reclined in the chair, but this time he was holding Astrid's hand.

All went well, and later that afternoon, when Bryce was alert, they did a few follow-up tests. He made appointments for more tests over the next few weeks with Dr. Goh and other medical professionals. Stevie and Dr. Goh walked with them to the lobby.

On the way to the parking garage, Astrid continued to look at her husband. "Oh, Bryce, are you really all right?"

"You fuckin' got that goddam right!"

She looked at him in alarm.

"Shit fuck goddam right!"

She looked at him again with sudden suspicion. She narrowed her eyes.

"Okay, okay, just kidding."

"Manaus? Manaus?? What were you thinking?" screeched Brenda. "I have sixteen mosquito bites, they're driving me fucking crazy, and I'm probably going to get yellow fever!"

"You were vaccinated. And don't be stupid! Manaus is an international center of trade. All kinds of people come here to do business. With just two languages, Portuguese and English, we're making a fortune."

"Dr. Nigel Grant-Elliott" dismissed his business partner with a wave of his hand.

"We're making fifty thousand a month off the cell-phone people alone. And every man who has had the Erotic Enhancement procedure tells me that he can't get it down."

"Well, I feel sorry for their poor girlfriends! Manaus is wet and dirty and crawling with insects. We could be doing so much better in Rio!"

"Brenda. Shut up and listen. I heard today that LOQUELA is opening a clinic in Rio."

"No!"

"So, we're staying right here, almost two thousand miles away, where we have an air-conditioned apartment with a beautiful view of the river and a nice balcony with mosquito nets and two maids and a driver."

"Maelí!" Brenda bellowed. "Bring me a caipirinha!"

She looked inquiringly at "Nigel." He nodded.

"Two caipirinhas!"

The Crab Pot, scene of so many griping sessions, confidences, courtships, impromptu support groups, gossipy conversations, and marital discords, was the place where Bryce and Astrid said a temporary good-bye to Justin and Kendra (ready to bloom at any moment), Ginnie, Ashley, and Hal.

Bryce and Astrid were going back to stay in Paris for a while, visit Rennes, and meet Astrid's extended family. Bryce was ready to converse with them in fluent and uninterrupted French. They were also preparing their applications to the University of Washington Department of History for admittance as graduate students for the following September. The plan – as far as they had one – was to go back to school, live in Seattle, and face the next decisions only when they had to. Life, they said, was an adventure. Not the kind of adventure that Marina enjoyed; adventures, they told one another, came in various flavors.

"It's going to be dull without you," said Ashley.

"You two have provided most of gossip around here that was worth gossiping about," said Ginnie. "With some help from Marina."

"You won't believe it," said Astrid, "but Marina and her pediatrician have set a date. Next summer we'll be going to their wedding."

Hal shook his head. "I don't know what the world is coming to. Marina settling down? What are we going to talk about?"

Astrid smiled. "A little dullness won't hurt you. Besides, it's somebody else's turn to provide small-town drama. We're retiring."

Justin shrugged. "Is drama so important? I think I could live happily ever after with no drama at all. Daily life is sufficient."

Kendra said "mmmmrrrggghhh."

Heads turned.

"What?"

"What is it, Sweetie?" asked Justin.

Kendra gulped. "You see over there, over in that other corner?"

"Yeah."

"That's Dr. Valerie."

"Yeah."

"You mind calling her over here? I'd like to talk with her."

"Okay, but what's the deal?"

Kendra clutched her bulging belly. "I think we're about to have some drama."

ABOUT THE AUTHOR

In the mid-nineties, with an M.A. in art history, Victoria Josslin began writing about art first for magazines, and then as a freelancer for a daily newspaper, where she wrote about any art show that came along, from Picasso ceramics to circus posters (true!). For the last ten years she has written for *Glass Quarterly* where she is now a contributing editor. *The Bookstore of Other Languages* is her first novel. She and her husband spend half the year near Seattle and the other half in Albuquerque.